# DAYS OF BROKEN OATHS

## MATT LARKIN

DAYS OF BROKEN OATHS

Runeblade Saga: Book Five

MATT LARKIN

This is a work of fiction. Names, characters, organizations, businesses, places, events and incidents either are the product of the author's imagination or are used fictitiously.

Published by Incandescent Phoenix Books

mattlarkinbooks.com

# CONTENTS

# PROLOGUE

*A* deep melancholy had settled upon Holmgard's people. It filled the air as Odin passed among them, disguised as an old man leaning upon a walking stick —hardly an affection, in truth, weary as he was. Despite the mist and the cold and the threat of war, in most towns, children played, craftsmen hawked their wares, and men and shieldmaidens boasted, wrestled, and drank.

Here, though, the stillness had settled upon the town like a weight, a stone pressing upon Odin's chest that made his steps feel heavy and slow as he approached Rollaugr's hall. Soon, Odin's throne would be complete and he would need tend to a great many tasks. This one, he had let fester long enough, like a rotting wound in his side.

For decades he had ignored the Miklagardians, thought them of even less consequence to his plans than the Serklanders. But they had begun to spread, and, more troubling were the revelations he'd uncovered about the source of their power. He needed something they had and, more, he needed to check their expansion so he could afford to focus his attention elsewhere.

The solution might well cost Odin several pieces he rather valued, but then, a piece one was unwilling to sacrifice had its utility greatly diminished. If his designs succeeded, though, he might well weaken the Miklagardians while managing to bring the last runeblade back to the North Realms in the process. A hefty chance, considering his visions were yet imperfect, and what he did foresee hinted at a dark urd for all involved.

But then, his visions had always hinted at a dark urd for poor Starkad.

And Odin had no more time in which to let caution guide his decisions.

The king's men showed Odin into Rollaugr's hall, the once glorious abode of Sigrlami, now seeming nigh to empty of thegns and warriors. The king himself did not sit upon his throne, but rather paced before the tables where some few gathered warriors sat. One, a woman, seemed a varulf, if Odin's instincts did not deceive him.

Among the Aesir, varulfur and berserkir had once held places of importance, but in Sviarland, and thus Holmgard, the creatures were rare, and oft considered more monster than human.

Also at the table sat a big man, large enough he might well have had jotunn blood. Rollaugr had collected allies almost as odd as Odin's own.

Rollaugr looked up at him, a frown creasing his brows, though it faded slightly in his moment of recognition. "Atrith? By Odin's spear, old man, you return after a great many winters. I had thought you gone forever."

Odin quirked a smile, always amused to hear others swear in his name, oft to his face, considering he so rarely revealed his true identity. "Not just yet."

Rollaugr waved in acknowledgement. "Perhaps I ought

to have known. You come only when the hour grows dark. And I cannot imagine it growing much darker than this." He looked to one of the men sitting on the benches. "Some of my advisors even suggest we ought to withdraw from these lands entirely, return to the homes of our ancestors in Sviarland. I might consider it, though word of Gylfi's death means I cannot imagine we are like to find peace there either."

Odin frowned. If the Holmgarders abandoned this foothold in Bjarmaland, either the Miklagardians or the jotunnar would claim the whole region within a few years. Then the winner would no doubt be pressing in on Kvenland and Sviarland, neither of which Odin could afford to lose as yet. "If you run from your foes now, men will call you craven, and you shall find no shelter in Sviarland. Least of all in this time of chaos when the kings war amongst themselves."

The varulf sniffed the air, eyeing Odin oddly. The problem with her kind was that his glamour didn't really disguise his scent. Fortunately, as far as he knew, this particular varulf had never seen him as Odin or anyone else other than Atrith. Maybe she'd catch a hint he was more than he appeared, but she was not like to be able to uncover the truth. Finally, she growled. "We need to press the offensive, sack Kaunos."

Rollaugr cast a withering gaze her way. "Even if such a foolhardy plan succeeded, it would cost us the better part of the warriors we yet have. Shall we send an invitation to Hymir or other jotunn lords? Ask them if they'd like to rule our land?"

Odin banged his walking stick on the floor, drawing all eyes. "Perhaps, my king, the solution lies not in more men, but in fewer."

"I do not follow you, old friend."

"A small crew, sent not merely to Kaunos, but to Miklagard itself when summer breaks."

Now Rollaugr scoffed. "And do what? Sue for peace?"

The varulf woman rose. "Kill Tanna ..."

Odin nodded. "Kill the lord who troubles you and thus send a message to the remaining Patriarchs. Tales say Tanna wields one of the lost runeblades of the Old Kingdoms. Defeat him despite this, claim the blade, and even Miklagard will be forced to take pause at Holmgard's power."

Rollaugr frowned at the varulf. "Your boldness will get you killed, Vebiorg. Whom am I to send upon such a mission?"

Odin opened his mouth to suggest Starkad—for he had few other pieces free at the moment, and Starkad was rather good at killing.

Before he could speak, the big man beat him to it. "Reckon Starkad Eightarms and Hervor Witchslayer could pull that off. I seen them do worse and live through it."

Interesting. So this big man had met Starkad. It was almost too perfect. Now, Odin need not even nudge Rollaugr in the right direction.

Rollaugr grunted. "And you believe they'd come if you asked them?"

"Reckon they would. Best I leave for Sviarland right quick though. They ain't always easy to find."

Ah. Well, a small nudge then. "I imagine I know where to find Eightarms," Odin said. "And yes, best you hurry. Summer is not so very far off now."

Rollaugr nodded at the big man, who rose and headed off. The king moved to Odin's side, put an arm around his shoulders, and guided him away from the others. Out of earshot of any save perhaps that varulf. "If this plan fails,

Tanna will come after us harder than ever. We will pay a price in blood and our kingdom will fall."

If the plan failed, Midgard would lose more than one small, dying kingdom on the edge of Bjarmaland. They'd be one step closer to losing Ragnarok.

But if they did naught, that future seemed certain.

Some gambits were worth risking losing a piece.

# PART I

Eleventh Moon
Year 31, Age of the Aesir

he Black Sea wasn't black—not exactly—but the waters were dark, and with the mist, more ominous than Hervor would've liked. Aught at all could've lurked beneath this sea. Serpents or worse, maybe. Hard to dismiss any of it as fancy anymore.

Not after what she'd seen in Pohjola.

Their foreign ship cut through the waters, a fair wind carrying them ever closer to Miklagard. The city loomed in the distance, barely visible through the vapors.

Squinting, Hervor could pick out domed spires and great arches and other strange constructions like naught she'd ever laid eyes on. And the closer they drew, the more intimidating those sights became. Like the South Realmers had built a city on a scale none since the Old Kingdoms had dared, if even them. Those outer walls rose up twenty, thirty feet easily, and Odin alone knew how thick.

Starkad's hand fell on her shoulder. "This place is little like aught you've known before."

Of that she had no doubt. Coming here might've been a mistake, but Starkad would not pass up this runeblade.

Maybe even the last runeblade, he'd confided, though Hervor had no idea how he knew that. Either way, even if Rollaugr hadn't offered such a fortune to do this, Starkad would've come. And that meant Hervor would've come too.

In her absence, though, who knew what vileness Orvar-Oddr would wreak upon Sviarland? Upon those she cared for. The draug had tormented her without end. Coming here meant leaving him free to do so for any number of moons more. But she couldn't tell Starkad that. Couldn't tell anyone, save maybe Höfund, who stood gaping dumbly at the approaching port.

"It's magnificent," the half-jotunn mumbled. "Ain't never imagined so many people all clustered up tight like that. Gotta wonder how they keep from tripping over each other."

She frowned and cast a glance back at the rest of Starkad's crew. Afrid Stonekicker stood a few feet from her, not even trying to hide her gaping at the approaching sight. Vebiorg was scowling like they sailed toward the gates of Hel itself. Who even knew what the others were thinking?

The ship itself was out of Kaunos, and her people were posing as merchants come to sell furs, with the captain and his sailors none the wiser as to their true purpose. Starkad and his men had loaded up crates of wolf pelts and snow bear skins all hunted from around Bjarmaland. A good enough plan to get in the city—assuming the port inspectors didn't take objection to the numerous weapons they bore.

Baruch assured them those inspectors would turn a blind eye to just about aught, provided Starkad handed over some silver coins.

Sure enough, as their ship docked at a pier, some official in black robes came bustling over, flanked by a pair of bodyguards. He strode on board the moment the crew had put down the gangplank. Immediately, he began spewing forth a stream of unintelligible foreign words. Was there a singular South Realmer tongue like Northern? Or did Miklagard and Valland have different languages?

She hadn't bothered to ask and it seemed pointless to pose the question now.

The official and the ship's captain exchanged words briefly, then the captain beckoned to Starkad. Hervor's lover tossed the official a jingling pouch. The official drew the strings to peer inside, nodded, and motioned for his guards to inspect the crates.

The two men popped one open, dug around in the wolf pelts. Muttered something to their employer. And just like that, they all turned and left. Didn't bother even checking the other crates, much less having a look at the passengers. Starkad's crew had swords over their shoulders, axes hanging from their belts ... Afrid had a damn spear in her hand.

Nigh as Hervor could tell, all these Miklagardians cared about was their damn silver.

"It makes the city run," Baruch said, as if reading her mind.

"You mean the whole place runs on greed."

The Miklagardian shrugged. "Word is you used to be a pirate, Witchslayer."

She flashed him a half grin. "Point taken."

The captain's crew set to unloading their own cargo, while Starkad ordered Höfund and Tveggi and the others to haul up the three crates. Maybe he actually intended to sell them and turn a profit, maybe he just thought they'd need the cover again later. Either way, the eight of them bid the captain farewell and trod out into the city.

Even in the harbor, it reeked. Ports always stank of brine and seaweed and refuse and such. But this one was too thick with humanity. Clusters of earthen buildings clumped together, practically on top of one another, some strung with colorful banners, other stained by the salty air. And every one of the narrow alleys between them was filled with gutters clogged with shit and stale piss and other unidentified filth.

Baruch turned about after the first alley, looked around as if confused.

"Lose the city?" Afrid asked. "I could probably point it out to you."

Indeed, the towering wall could be seen from pretty much anywhere.

Baruch scowled at the young shieldmaiden. "Unless you can walk through walls, I thought you might want to go in the gate." He pointed off down another street. "Which is that way."

"You sure?" the young shieldmaiden prodded. "We could give you a bit to think it over."

"I was a child when last I was here, younger than you, if slightly more mature."

Hervor quirked a smile and shook her head.

"The crates are fucking heavy," Tveggi complained.

"It's this way," Baruch repeated. He led them through a winding circuit, eventually opening out into a main walkway crowded with people bustling in and out of a great archway at least fifteen feet tall.

Hervor had been wrong before. Those walls were closer to forty feet high. And from the space within—lined with guards holding halberds—more than ten feet thick. The gates stood open, but double wooden portcullises hung above both sides. Starkad had been right when he said no army was taking this city by force.

Hervor swallowed at the sight.

Starkad though, he just strode right up to the gate, forcing everyone to follow. As usual, really.

Baruch exchanged a couple of words with a guard, passed him something—more coins?—and then waved everyone on. "Welcome to Miklagard."

The main gate let out onto an even more crowded street. All the buildings in here were the color of dirt, save for the towering spires and palaces in the distance. Those put to shame the halls of the mightiest kings of the North Realms. Hel, it was hard to imagine Asgard itself being bigger.

And this city just kept going on and on.

They passed into a market clogged with vendors hawking clothes, fruits, incense, spices, and Odin alone knew what else. Men with skin so dark it seemed almost black. Men with pale skin like her own. And the greater part of them with the deeper skin tones like Baruch. Merchants from all over Midgard, it seemed.

"Fuck me," Afrid mumbled. "Didn't know this many people lived in all Midgard."

All this splendor, but something was missing. Hervor couldn't quite say what, but something for sure. Vebiorg was turning about too, nose wrinkled like she'd caught some foulness in the air. Exotic scents and strange meats cooking overwhelmed the stench of human waste in the market, but maybe Vebiorg's nose was more sensitive, given her nature.

"Torches," Hervor blurted, suddenly realizing what was missing. There were hardly any torch poles and no obvious braziers. "How are they keeping the mists back without torches?"

"The walls are high," Win offered. The prince didn't seem entirely convinced by his own suggestion though. Nor should he ... the port hadn't been over-saturated with mists either.

Hervor frowned. Something was unnatural about Miklagard, even if she could not quite say what.

"Win," Starkad said. "Take Baruch and find some place we can sleep. Somewhere we won't attract attention, where we can work, plan. Hervor, you and Vebiorg see about getting us some food."

"We don't speak the language," Vebiorg objected.

Starkad handed her another pouch of silver. "Fair universal communication." He looked to the others. "The rest of you, scout the market in small groups. Get a feel for it. We're going to need to know our way around. If you find those who speak our tongue, you can ask a few questions about Tanna, but be discreet. We don't want him to know we're coming."

"I stay with my prince," Tveggi said.

Starkad shrugged and motioned them on.

Hervor frowned. Vebiorg had already started off toward a vendor selling roasted meat on a stick. She trotted off after the varulf woman. "Do you even know what that is?"

Vebiorg sniffed, cocked her head to the side. "Rat."

Hervor blanched, not bothering to hide her disgust.

The varulf grinned at her. "It's hot and it's fresh. I don't think you can ask for too much more in this strange land."

That only reinforced Hervor's doubts about whether they should have even come here. No matter how she tried, she could not shake the unease that had settled upon her the moment she'd walked through those gates.

$\mathscr{B}$aruch had found them an apartment in the maze-like warrens behind the market. It was just one room and would've been cramped for a family of four or five. With nine grown people, they were practically jammed up against the walls like it was a fucking tomb, especially with those crates taking up one corner.

Starkad misliked this whole city, but these confines most of all. He could've sat by the window, except that let in the stench of human waste lining the narrow alleys around the building.

Here, close to the fire pit, at least the smoke cut down on the reek. Besides, Vebiorg had kept her head hanging out the window almost constantly. Starkad preferred giving her space. As much space as possible.

Hervor had her back pressed up against his and he could almost feel the vibrations of her teeth grinding. No need to even ask how she felt about Miklagard.

Afrid groaned, scrunched up in a corner. "Why in the frozen wastes of Niflheim would people choose to live like this? It's like jamming yourself into a beehive."

"You prefer the mists?" Baruch asked, though from his face he didn't seem sure of the answer himself. He sniffed. "People don't talk about the emperor much. Nobody's ever even seen him as far as I know. But there's tales—whispered, mind, when there aren't too many to overhear—they say he keeps out the mists himself."

"Troll shit," Afrid said. "No man holds back the mists."

"Don't know that he is a man. Here, people figure he's ... like a god. Like the Aesir, maybe."

"Do not compare these foreigners to the Aesir," Win snapped.

Starkad's frown only deepened. The Aesir lived without the mists because of the World Tree, not any power of their own. Some of them might've been immortal, but he'd not have preferred to think of them as gods. Maybe least of all since he'd lost his chance at immortality among them.

They were men and women, arrogant ones. But he could not deny they had powers, strange gifts. Odin especially. Starkad's dreams had been plagued with cryptic visions of Miklagard ever since they left Kaunos. He'd seen the city in his mind before they got here. Worse, then, to arrive and find it matched his visions. Such made it hard to dismiss his dreams.

Odin was fucking with him again. Or ... warning him.

It wasn't words with the Ás though. Naught so explicit nor useful. No, Odin had to keep up his mysteries. So he taunted Starkad with shadows, with the hint that something ancient dwelled in Miklagard. Something even Odin didn't fully understand ... and maybe feared. That alone was enough to give a man pause. Odin, who'd faced Niflung sorcerers and the Vanir and linnorms and who knew what else, seemed apprehensive of this place.

Had Odin sent Starkad here? Starkad had thought his

own choices had brought him, but as long as Odin kept messing with his dreams, how could he be sure? Maybe it didn't matter overmuch though. He was here now.

"As best we can surmise so far," Win said, "twelve Patriarchs rule Miklagard. They alone claim to have seen the emperor. If we assume for the moment this emperor exists, his sole province appears to be preventing outright war between the Patriarchs, and only just, at that."

Baruch nodded. "The Patriarchs themselves aren't seen much either, for that matter. Tanna is one of them, though. Each Patriarch is responsible for a district in the city as well as a prefecture of the empire at large."

"Pre-what now?" Höfund grumbled.

"The largest divisions of the empire," Baruch answered. "Kaunos is in Tanna's prefecture."

"So," Hervor said. "Which district of the city does he rule?"

Baruch shrugged.

Now the shieldmaiden pulled away from Starkad's back to stare at the Miklagardian. "You don't *know*?"

"I had seven, maybe eight winters when I was taken into slavery and sent to work farms around Kaunos. And before that, I didn't spend my time mingling with the lords of the city. I spent it begging, scrounging, and stealing just enough food to avoid starving to death. I spent it running from shopkeepers and guards. And sometimes getting caught. Being forced to ..." Baruch grimaced, then spat into the fire.

Fjolvor scooted closer and put her arm around her husband. She never said much, really. Baruch leaned against her, glowering.

"Not so happy to be back here, then?" Afrid asked.

"No."

"Something is wrong with this city," Vebiorg said, still not drawing back inside the window.

Baruch scoffed. "A great many things are wrong with any settlement so large. Shoved into tight confines, humans become more like animals."

That did get Vebiorg looking at him, head cocked sideways.

If Baruch appreciated the irony of talking to a varulf about men acting like animals, he gave no sign of it.

Starkad cleared his throat. "So what we need is more information. We'll sleep here tonight and use the morning to scout the city. The nine of us together might attract too much attention, so we'll go in two groups. I'll lead one and Hervor will lead the other."

Win bristled. "As a prince of Holmgard—"

"As a member of the crew you'll do what I godsdamned tell you to. Rollaugr hired me to lead this quest. If you could've done it on your own, you would've. You'll go with Hervor, Höfund, Tveggi, and Vebiorg. Learn whatever you can." Starkad looked to Baruch. "You're with me. Fjolvor and Stonekicker too."

The prince scowled at him, then rose and stomped over to where Vebiorg stood at the window. The two of them began whispering to one another. No doubt whining about Starkad. He couldn't say as he much cared.

Hervor leaned in close to his ear. "I appreciate the honor of command, but I might've preferred to stay by your side."

"I need someone I can trust to watch over the others. Win's got too much pride and Vebiorg is like to be driven by her nature."

"Huh. Suppose so. Listen." She rubbed his arm. "When this is done ... We still need to talk. Think about where we're going from here."

"Wherever the next adventure is."

She groaned. "You jest? We'll be rich after this. Surely it's enough for you?"

He shook his head. "You know it doesn't work that way for me. And I'm not having this conversation again. Get some sleep. The sooner we finish this, the sooner we can leave Miklagard."

Hervor grimaced, mumbled something under her breath, and crawled as far away as the narrow confines allowed.

Starkad shut his eyes. They'd taken oaths to stay by each other's side in all their journeys. But she'd known who he was back then. Known well his curse would never let him rest nor hold wealth.

No peace. No children.

Just the road. And them.

And for a little while, he dared to believe that might be enough for her.

# 3

*W*hatever Starkad had said about placing Hervor in charge of a team, it sure as fuck seemed he just wanted to push her away. After all they'd been through, still he couldn't open up about what went on inside his head. No, but she could harbor a guess.

Bastard.

Never listened to her. Not really.

Höfund tromped along beside her as she strolled the market, drawing stares everywhere they went. "Something I been meaning to talk with you on. Ain't had much chance, really." He glanced back at where Vebiorg was trailing behind them, probably not out of earshot given her nature, but maybe Höfund didn't know that.

Win and Tveggi were across the street, talking to a street vendor. The prince was not nigh so fluent in Miklagardian as Baruch, but better than the rest of them. Which wasn't hard, really.

"See, the thing of it is," Höfund said. "Right, well, best be out with it. A while back, I came to be thinking—"

"Focus on the reason we're here."

"Oh. Uh, sure."

Maybe it would've been best to have out with it. Tell him things would never go the way he wanted and he might as well look elsewhere. Except, the thought of seeing the big man's grimace didn't sit well with her. Besides, right now, she really *did* need him focused on the mission. Höfund was the strongest of their crew and she couldn't well afford to lose his loyalty.

Win trudged over to where Hervor and the others had stopped. "None of the locals know exactly which lord rules which district. Apparently the lords don't readily show themselves. Maybe they fear being murdered for their despotism. So they work through an interminable chain of intermediary officials."

Hervor sighed. "You mean we've been wasting our time."

"Perhaps not. There's a primicerius's office up the street, and, even if the official does not directly tie back to Tanna, he is more like to know of the lords than any common man."

"A what's office?" Höfund asked.

"A primicerius."

Höfund chuckled. "Sounds like a beast what needs slaying. Got an office though. Ain't heard that before."

At least he still had his sense of humor. "What exactly is a primicerius?" Hervor asked.

Tveggi glanced around as if this was all some big secret. Hand on his sword hilt. Ever watchful of his prince.

"A primicerius," Win said, "is a subordinate to a tribune. Nigh as I can tell, tribunes are officials who administer the city on behalf of the Patriarchs."

All right ... "I thought the Patriarchs ran it on behalf of this emperor?"

"Odin alone knows how many titles fall in this chain. What is of consequence here, though, is that this official receives plebeian inquiries directly. That is to say, we can talk to him ourselves, this very day, assuming we're willing to pay enough to push ahead of other claimants."

Hervor didn't bother asking what plebeians were. Not only was the city laid out in a maze, it was as if the inhabitants had worked their whole social structure into a twisted knot to mirror the landscape. "Just lead the way."

As it turned out, "this very day" was used rather liberally. The primicerius's office was practically drowning in people waiting to plead their cases. All of whom had probably laid down bribes to get ahead of the others. Which meant Hervor had been standing around for at least four hours before the man's assistant even called them in.

Didn't really leave her in a gracious mood.

Nor did the man's sneer when he looked upon her and her crew. The pompous little shit sat behind a table laden with books, ink vials, and no less than a dozen coin purses. Plus some construction of beads that slid along a rod. A child's toy?

"North Realmers," the man said, in a grating accent. "What do you want?"

Hervor stifled her shock at hearing him speak—if you could call it that—her own tongue. "Where do we find Tanna?" she demanded.

"Diplomacy," Win urged, motioning with his hands downward.

Hervor rolled her eyes. "Please ... tell us where the fuck to find Tanna."

Win groaned, rubbed his temples. "Primicerius. We're lately out of Kaunos and have come in the hopes of establishing a mutually beneficial trade agreement for both our peoples. We need to arrange an audience with the Patriarch and thus require directions to his district."

There was that sneer back on the Miklagardian's face. Would it seem less obnoxious if she cut off his nose? Might soften his features a bit.

"The Patriarch does not see merchants himself."

Win looked around a moment, then leaned on the table, pulling another jingling pouch from inside his shirt. "We'd be more than willing to plead our case to his immediate junior, if you could but direct us to the right place."

The Miklagardian's sneer eased, ever so slightly. Almost haltingly, he reached for the pouch, then drew it open to look inside.

"Tanna's tower is nigh to the river, east side. Call upon the tribune there. Now, if that shall be all?"

Win motioned to Tveggi, who produced yet another pouch from inside *his* shirt and dropped it on the table. How much coin had the prince *brought*? And did he intend to give it all away in bribes in their first two days in the city?

"So," Win said, "supposing someone wanted to see the lord himself, how would that someone go about that?"

Huh. What exactly was the price for revealing information about one's lord?

The official opened the second pouch as well, brow rising slightly. "Supposing that were the case, the person might find the Patriarch has a private palace, but spends most of his time in the tower. That he not only works there, but often lives there, in highest reaches, if stories hold true."

Well, whatever the price, the wretched little man seemed more than willing to sell out his lord. Any oaths of loyalty he'd ever taken clearly meant troll shit to him.

Hervor didn't bother trying to keep the disgust from her face.

Shaking her head, she turned and left, trailed by the others.

Outside, Win turned about, orienting himself, before focusing on a spire rising above the city in the distance. While countless towers dotted the skyline, some seemed substantially larger and more elaborately decorated than others. Each a tower of a Patriarch? "It's that one," Win said.

More than a short jaunt from where they were staying, by Hervor's estimate. "We need to let Starkad know before we do aught else."

𝕊

HERVOR SAT with her back to the wall, watching the door in their cramped apartment. Vebiorg was beside her, while Höfund and Win appeared caught up in stories about friends lost in the recent strikes against Miklagard. Tveggi was with them, though the old man mostly just nodded along rather than speaking.

"So," Vebiorg said.

Hervor had almost wanted to move away when the varulf had slumped down beside her. Maybe she wanted the woman along for her strengths, but still. Didn't mean she wanted the savage creature close at hand.

"So," Hervor answered, not looking at the other woman.

"You've the scent of blood on you."

"You can smell that?" Hervor had washed a good many times since last she'd slain anyone.

Vebiorg snorted. "More a sense of it. Plenty of shield-maidens, they've fought, bled, killed. But some of us, we've seen more battles than others. Maybe too many. I get that sense from you. Strange, for one so young. How many winters have you seen?"

She hardly thought about it anymore. Her life had been chaos for so many ... "Twenty-six now, I think. Counting this one just past." And summer here was hot enough she almost missed the winter. "What of you?"

"Not sure. Forty, maybe."

"*Forty*? I'd not have taken you for even my age."

Vebiorg shrugged. "My kind age more slowly. I can remember when the Vanir were still the gods. Later, I was fair young when Sigrlami was king. The uh ... the pack died. The king took me as a slave. Used me to keep watch of his hall while he slept. Used me for ... his desires sometimes. But he died, too, some few years later."

Killed by Arngrim, Hervor's grandfather. Hervor kept her face studiously expressionless.

"Rollaugr's father took the throne, offered me freedom if I fought for him. Seemed a fair trade. Can't say the other warriors ever took well to me, though. You ever have people look at you with fear, even when they're your own allies?"

"Sure." Hervor had rather cultivated such a reputation on purpose in her pirating days. "I used to dress as a man, figured it'd help to keep my enemies scared and my allies in line. That they'd take me more seriously and I'd be less like to need to draw a blade."

"Why'd you stop?"

Hervor rocked her head gently against the wall. Honestly, she couldn't even say exactly *when* she'd stopped trying to be Hervard. "The last time ... I guess the last time was around when I met Höfund."

"Wanted to be a woman for him?"

Hervor snorted and Vebiorg chuckled. "Let's call it a

coincidence. After that, I was in this place, this valley in Jotunheim."

"Troll shit."

"Swear on Odin's almighty stones."

"Uh, on what now?"

Hervor grinned. "Place was like a vision of Niflheim, ghosts included. Just me and Starkad there, and us trying to fend off the dead. And I just … I don't know. By the time I made it out, I was kind of … tired."

"Fighting the dead will do that, I hear."

"No, I mean to say, I was tiring of the life I'd led before. I'd been a raider, a pirate, a … murderer, more than once. I'd fought draugar and finfolk and svartalfar."

"And ghosts."

"Yes." Saying it all aloud, she couldn't fathom how she wasn't dead ten times over. Maybe that was the reason behind the supreme fatigue. "Maybe I didn't … want to be the person I'd been up till then. A real bitch, actually."

Vebiorg chuckled. "You're talking to a female wolf, mind you."

"You're saying you're not a bitch, then?"

"A right terror when I don't get my night meal timely. Three things you never take from a wolf. Their food, their mate, or … their pack."

One of which Vebiorg had already lost.

Hervor sighed. "I had some friends a few years back. Couple of other shieldmaidens. A pack of varulfur down in Skane killed one of them. Maybe the same pack that took down Gylfi."

"Huh. That why Starkad hates me?"

"He doesn't hate you."

"I can smell his loathing."

Hervor turned to look at her more directly. Could she

really? "Anyway, no, Starkad wasn't even there when it happened. With him ... a varulf killed his mother." One of the few bits of his past he'd actually shared with her, after his ordeal with the mara.

Vebiorg grunted. "Never been to Sviarland. Didn't do either one of those things. And I didn't choose to let the wolf inside me, either. Eightarms's scorn grows tiresome."

"He's ... complicated."

"More complicated than a woman half possessed by a Moon spirit? Always losing control of my rage and lust? Torn between animal and human sides?"

Hervor ran that over in her mind. "Honestly? Maybe more complicated still."

Vebiorg raised an eyebrow at that, but said naught more.

IT WAS WELL into the afternoon before Starkad and his team returned. Baruch and Fjolvor slumped down by the crates, him seeming to try to comfort her. Woman was clearly miserable. Not that Hervor could much blame her. Miklagard was overcrowded, filthy, and corrupt. And Fjolvor hadn't wanted to come *before* seeing all that.

The city beat Pohjola or many of the other far-flung places Hervor had visited, if only because no horrors of the Otherworlds were trying to kill her.

Win fell into explaining what they'd learned to Starkad and the others, with Starkad asking only the occasional questions.

Finally, their leader scratched his beard and looked around the room. "Any attempt to make a meeting with Tanna is like to fail. From what Win has said, the lord has underlings to handle his tasks."

"So we meet with one of those arse buckets," Afrid said. "And when they start talking like donkeys, gut them and then search for Tanna."

"Imbecile," Tveggi mumbled.

"Sorry," Afrid said. "I couldn't make out your words over the sound of some old man farting."

Baruch held up a hand to each of them, before either took it to blows. "Anyone working for Tanna is like to have numerous guards. Even if we overcame them—and they might not allow us weapons inside—we'd then have the tower alerted to our presence, searching for us. Total chaos."

"Chaos is an opportunity," Afrid offered.

Starkad shook his head. "Too risky. I see but one option before us. We wait until well after dark, then scale the walls once no one is out and about to see us. Hervor and I pulled off something similar to kill the king of Njarar."

Oh, Odin's stones. Not more climbing. "We nigh died in Njarar. One of our men *did* fall to his death in the process."

"He was a drunk," Starkad snapped at her. "And your complaints hardly help our situation."

Hervor clapped her mouth shut. Was that how it was going to be now?

Fine. If he wanted to climb, she would fucking climb.

And afterward, they'd be having a godsdamned talk.

# 4

Four Moons Ago

So little remained of the home Hervor had once known. Grandfather had but a few servants left, and a single pair of warriors. Perhaps Hrethel thought himself generous to allow the fallen jarl even that much, but Hervor could hardly forgive the slight. Nor had Grandfather recovered from his mistreatment at Hrethel's hands.

Wrapped in a blanket, the old man wheezed on his chair —one could hardly call it a throne with no jarldom left— then set to coughing. A fit of it seized him and he shook, trembling, before finally hacking up a glob of phlegm onto the floor. She didn't much want to believe the thickness had him, but the signs seemed clear enough.

Hervor flinched, trying to cover her reaction. She stood before him in his ruined hall, alone for the moment. The fields and towns had been taken by Hrethel, and this empty compound now served as a pitiful reminder of a past she'd disdained.

Until it was gone.

Gunther was dead. The other thegns, too, save a few who'd taken up with new lords now.

Some maybe Hrethel had driven away. Others had turned up dead in Deeppine, torn to pieces. Grandfather had blamed bandits. Hervor knew better. The Arrow's Point would never be done with her. One by one, he hunted and destroyed everyone she'd ever known.

Probably only left this hall in peace because he knew her grandfather was dying a slow, awful death.

"I just …" Grandfather wheezed. "Just want … what's best for you."

Hervor frowned. Not long ago she'd have sneered at that. Would've chafed at the reins she'd have accused him of placing on her. Petulant bitch that she was. "I know that."

She *should've* known it before he was dying. Should've done a lot of things, maybe. He'd always been the one extending his hand, trying to let the past lie. And she'd wasted uncounted winters being too much the fool to see it.

Grandfather cleared his throat. "An offer came for your hand."

Hervor shook her head. Grandfather may have wanted the best for her, but she wasn't interested in marrying any man save perhaps Starkad, and he had made clear he'd not wed her nor anyone else.

"Just … listen. This Höfund is a prince, son of a foreign king."

Höfund? Odin's stones. Höfund was a king's son all right —the bastard son of a godsdamned jotunn king in Utgard. He was a friend, true. Shit, once she'd even lain with him and Starkad both together. But marry him, leave Starkad? No. Never. "Even if I fancied him, I am bound to Starkad."

Grandfather snorted, coughed, and shook his head. "Eightarms hasn't given you ... aught but grief. Nor will he. What future do you ... see with him?"

Her only future, really. She'd made her choices and given her oaths and she wasn't the kind to walk away from either. Starkad had spent the better part of a year convalescing here, once he'd been strong enough to leave Gylfi's hall.

Väinämöinen had been long gone by the time Hervor had returned from Kvenland and found Starkad a wreck of his former self. Her lover was blind in one eye and half blind in the other. Weakened, walking like both his legs were broken. Grimacing like every breath was pain. Best the song-crafter had been gone—elsewise, Hervor might've gutted him for his part in all that.

And with no völva and hardly a servant, Hervor had done her best to ease Starkad back to health. Maybe she'd gotten nigh to that, but there was no going back to what he'd been. Same as Hervor, really. She wouldn't ever have full use of her right arm. Some things you had to come to terms with.

Finally, she shrugged again. "I made my decision long ago."

"Hervor ... you are the last of our line. If you ..." He broke into another fit of coughing, but she could well guess what he'd intended to say. If she didn't bear an heir, their family ended with her. It wasn't like the thought had never crossed her mind. She just didn't have a half decent answer for it.

One of the inner doors creaked open, and Toril poked her head in.

"What is it?" Hervor snapped at the servant.

"There's men outside, Jarl. Say they've come to call on Eightarms." Grandfather wasn't jarl of aught more than a ruin, but Toril just kept up with the title all the same. The woman was some few winters older than Hervor and had always been around. Served Jarl Bjalmar her whole life. Now, it seemed she couldn't accept things had changed.

Then again, neither could Hervor. "What men?"

"Aun of Upsal, he says he is. Got a pair of warriors with him, too."

Aun was an Yngling, the former king of Upsal. Didn't reign long, though, before his enemies showed up and took the throne right out from under him. Maybe because he was a craven and a weakling. Still, he'd sheltered her and Starkad a few winters back, so she could hardly turn him away now. A woman had to remember her debts. "Where's Starkad?"

Toril fidgeted. "Out in the yard, flailing away." As usual.

Hervor glanced at Grandfather, but he'd already fallen asleep, head slumped to one side. "Fine. Bring them into the courtyard. And then stoke the braziers in here, make sure Grandfather is warm enough."

Winter had already settled in. The old man couldn't afford to fall too cold.

She made her way out of the hall and into the yard. Hrethel's forces had breached and burned much of the outer wall. When Hervor had gotten back, she'd helped them patch it herself. The shoddy work wouldn't have kept raiders out, but it served well enough to hold back the worst of the mist and wolves and such.

Starkad spun and twisted out there, whipping both swords around with *almost* his old speed, if not quite his old surety of foot. Hervor approached, careful not to draw too nigh on his blind side. Sneaking up on him was like to get her killed.

"Starkad."

Panting, he turned to her, and let his swords droop.

"Aun is here."

Even as she spoke, Toril opened the main gate for Aun and his two men, if you could call them that. One of them was young enough he probably just barely qualified. Hervor squinted at him. Actually, that looked like one of Aun's sons, if she wasn't mistaken. Grown a bit since last she'd laid eyes on him.

Starkad sheathed his blades and walked to meet Aun, slow and steady, maybe trying to conceal how winded he was.

"Starkad Eightarms," Aun said. "King Gylfi said I'd find you here, but I almost didn't dare to hope. You've all but disappeared of late."

Starkad scratched his beard. "King Aun."

Hervor rolled her eyes. At this point, Aun was even less a king than her grandfather was a jarl.

The king hesitated, as if expecting someone to say more. To invite him in for a meal, perhaps. It would've been the custom, but Hervor had next to naught to offer him, and if he couldn't well see that by looking around, he was twice the fool.

"Ah," Aun said after a moment. "So, I suppose I best come to the reason I'm here."

Seemed wise. Hervor barely managed not to say it aloud though.

"Well," the former king said. "You've no doubt heard about Ole the Strong out of Reidgotaland. He's a cousin to King Hrothgar and fancies himself a prince. So he set about trying to make his own kingdom ..."

"And wound up taking yours," Hervor finished. She had no patience for a man who couldn't even admit his own weakness. Or cowardice, really, since he'd fled at the first sign of the battle going against his men, from what she'd heard.

"He did, in fact. And I've come to hire you to deal with him."

Starkad spat. "Murder him, you mean. Thing is, I know Ole. I fought beside him some years back. And now you'd have me hunt and kill him."

Aun fidgeted. "Yes, well, you know me, as well, and I've offered hospitality and shelter to you and yours in the past."

"And we'll pay you well," one of the other men said. "Not just silver, but gold. A lot of gold."

"Who is this?" Starkad asked.

Aun glanced at the other man. "Lennius of Sjaelland."

Another Reidgotalander? A rival of Ole's, perhaps. And that meant Aun was dragging Starkad into a feud between princes of another country. Not an ideal place to be.

"Starkad ..." Hervor said.

He stiffened slightly, but didn't look at her. Of course he didn't. Because he damn well knew what she'd say. "How much gold?"

"Your weight in it," Lennius said.

Hervor blew out a breath. That much gold ... well, it could turn around even their flagging fortunes. Still, she'd spent years trying to eradicate the Ynglings. She might have called her vengeance sated, but urd truly had a wicked sense of humor to see her now trying to put one back on his throne.

"I'll do it," Starkad said.

Hervor wanted to be able to smile at the thought of so

much gold. Wanted to, but then, was Starkad really ready for this? Or was he doing this as much to prove to himself he still could?

Much as she needed the wealth, none of this sat well with Hervor.

## 5

"We cannot well climb in daylight," Starkad said, "so we'll scout the area until then. Best to be as familiar as possible with these streets and alleys in case aught goes wrong."

Hervor rolled her eyes. Naught had *ever* gone wrong with any of Starkad's mist-mad plans, had it? No, unless you counted a few dead allies here and there. No, but still, they'd climb the damn tower, murder a lord of the city, and get out without the slightest trouble.

"Small groups," the man said. "Avoid attracting notice as much as possible. Hervor, you go with Win."

"I go with my prince," Tveggi said, standing not a foot away from Win. Damn bodyguard probably helped Win piss most days, too.

Starkad shrugged. "Fine. Scout the northeast side, close to the river. If we have to flee the city, we want the way to the harbor clear." He turned to the others. "Höfund and Vebiorg, scout the northwestern regions. We shouldn't need to retreat there, but best to be certain. Baruch and Fjolvor will take the southeast, along the river. That's our likely route back to our apartment, if all goes as planned. Stone-kicker and I will take the southwest."

Hervor folded her arms and glared at Starkad. Wanted to go with the younger shieldmaiden, did he? Or just wanted to avoid the fight he had to know was coming. Either way, the bastard had to know he was making it all worse on himself. "Come on," she snapped at Win, trudging off before even waiting to see if he followed.

GREAT SHIPS SAILED THE RIVER, a half dozen of them in sight. Maybe more out in the mist, too. They were bigger than Northern longships, bulkier. Slower, probably, though she'd guess any outfitted for war could hold a troll-sized crew of warriors.

She'd seen more than a few Miklagardian soldiers passing along the streets on the way toward the tower. Men clad in heavier armor than aught she'd seen elsewhere. Like warped metal plates layered on top of one another, covering their chest and abdomen in a godsdamned turtle shell. Wonder they could move in all that. And since it left their legs exposed while still slowing them, it didn't seem the most practical.

Others had mail, though. More sensible protection as far as she was concerned. Made her miss her own. Starkad had insisted they leave their armor in the apartment for fear of attracting too much notice. Might've been right about it, but still, she misliked being in foreign lands with naught between her flesh and a blade but her clothes.

They'd seen a fair number of these patrols both days. Made her worry on their chances.

"It's a strange thing," Win said, watching the ships

himself. "Walking in the midst of enemies I've fought most of my life. I would never question the will of the Aesir, but still, I cannot say I much like coming here."

"The Aesir?" Hervor asked. "What have they got to do with this?"

"The gods guide the urd of men and women. It is only through their will we find ourselves drawn to these far shores."

Hervor snorted, earning herself a glare from both Win and Tveggi. Finally she shook her head. "Come on."

They skirted the river, passing close to the tower itself. Standing below it, its sheer scale left her feeling like a mouse. It had to be fifty feet across, maybe more, all made from tightly locked gray stones. The thing ended in a slight dome, with a spike rising up out of it like it meant to pierce the clouds. Only the upper regions nigh to the dome had windows, though below those a ring of arrow slots dotted the surface. Hard to judge the height, but she'd guess at least a hundred feet.

She grunted. "How in Hel's frozen underworld does he expect us to climb this?"

Win flinched. "Do not mention the name of the dark goddess."

That drew a snort from her. "You're worse than Starkad. Afraid she'll hear you?"

The prince frowned. "You've known him long, yes? Starkad Eightarms?"

"Ugh. Seven winters, I suppose."

"And yet, you two have still not wed?"

Hervor glowered. "Focus on the damn tower. We need a way in." She pushed on, continuing to make a circuit of it.

Win followed, mercifully silent. The sun was already dipping low on the horizon, and night would settle in within the hour. And still she had no guess as to how they'd climb this. The surface wasn't totally smooth, but she didn't fancy her chances of trying to climb up without any solid foot or handholds.

Win pointed to the windows. "We could try throwing a grapple into a window."

Hervor grunted, having to crane her neck to even see that high. "Not even Höfund could throw that far. Not straight up."

"What about from an adjacent rooftop?"

Huh. Maybe. That would substantially close the gap, assuming they could find the right roof. The tallest of the buildings rose maybe forty feet up themselves. Maybe the half-jotunn could do it. Whether he could do it quietly enough, Odin alone knew. "It's the best I can think of."

"Trust in Odin to guide us."

"Sure." Odin hadn't done all that much for her, so far as Hervor knew, but Win didn't seem to want to hear that.

"My prince," Tveggi said.

"Yes?"

"Have you noticed how few people are about here?"

Hervor turned, looked. Indeed, where the streets had seemed crowded an hour ago, now they were almost empty. Most of those she did see were scrambling into the nearby buildings, throwing shutters, slamming doors.

She frowned. "You'd think a place that manages to keep out the mist would remain more lively at night."

"One would think," Win agreed. "But who can say over-much about their customs."

Tveggi was turning about, slowly scanning each alley like he expected a troll to come rampaging down one any moment.

Hervor clapped the old man on his arm.

He flinched, hand going for the sword over his shoulder for a bare instant. Didn't meet her gaze, though. Embarrassed by his reaction, maybe. "Best we find the others before it gets full dark."

True enough. Hervor cast a last look at the massive tower. She was not looking forward to this.

❧

AS IT TURNED OUT, Starkad agreed with Win's plan to scale an adjacent building. The rougher stonework and occasional windowsill made doing so easier than climbing the tower would've been.

Nevertheless, Hervor grunted, panting, as she pulled herself up over the lip of the roof. It was flat—praise Odin—and she scrambled up onto her knees. Missing a finger on her right hand ... And that shoulder had never recovered from a wound years ago. All of it made climbing one of her least favorite activities.

The others pulled themselves up as well. Nine men and women, crouching on a rooftop in the middle of Miklagard itself. Up here, she had a better view of the city. A whole string of rooftops of differing heights ran for miles, it seemed, breaking up only because of the river and the Black Sea.

Some of the roofs were angled. Some had plate-like shingles. Some stretched along great distances, a hundred feet or more. Many had a slight blue tinge, more ominous in the night.

Speaking of which, the mist *had* thickened a bit during the evening. It flowed around the buildings, rising a few feet off the ground in swirling clouds.

"Place seems worser and worser," Höfund mumbled. "Kinda makes me miss Jotunheim."

She wouldn't go that far. "Can you get the grapple up there, on the balcony around the dome?"

Höfund gnawed on his lip, staring up at it. "Reckon I can. Ain't had overmuch practice on that sort of thing, though."

Afrid snorted. "Where'd you learn our language? From a deaf child?"

The big man looked at her. Hervor couldn't say whether he was offended, but she gave serious consideration to punching Afrid. "Well," Höfund said. "Me, I mostly learned it from Father. Figure he got it from a handful of human slaves like yourself. Them what he didn't eat or rape to death, that is."

Afrid opened her mouth, her slight grin rapidly disappearing when no one laughed. Probably wondering if Höfund was serious. Slowly, horrifyingly, realizing he was.

A slight smirk crept upon Hervor's face.

"Make your best shot," Starkad said. He looked around, probably scanning the streets for anyone who might see if someone stood on the roof. "Do it now."

"Right then." Höfund rose up, hefted the grapple and began to swing it round in a circle. Faster, until its whoosh whistled through the air. Until its passing ruffled Hervor's hair. Then he strode forward a step and flung the grapple.

The metal prongs clanked against the side of the balcony, then fell down to clatter on the cobblestone street. Hervor flinched. That had been graceless.

Höfund crouched down among the others, all now pressing themselves even lower against the roof. "Uh. Sorry 'bout that. Could've gone better, I reckon."

Starkad scrambled to the edge of the roof, grabbed the

rope, and began drawing up the grapple with remarkably little noise. Then he turned, looked about. "No sign of patrols anywhere. Like they don't even watch the streets at night."

Vebiorg sniffed. "Something is amiss in this place."

"No doubt," Starkad said, then turned to Höfund. "Try again."

The big man rose up again, twirling once more. Another heave. Once more, it smacked against the tower and plummeted to the street.

"Odin's godsdamned stones," Hervor mumbled.

"W-what did you say?" Win sputtered. "How can you ... how dare you invoke the name of the—"

"Give me the damn thing," Vebiorg snapped, snatching the grapple line from Höfund. "Oaf."

Hervor flinched at the varulf's tone, but she wasn't entirely wrong.

"Right then," Höfund said, slumping down on his arse and gnawing at his lip once more.

Vebiorg twirled the grapple, then flung it. It clanked over the lip of the balcony and she jerked it into place. The varulf smirked. "Who's first?"

"I am," Starkad said. "Secure the line."

The varulf looked around the empty roof. "To what?"

"Swing to the tower," Fjolvor offered.

Starkad shook his head. "No one else would be able to follow. The line won't reach down to the street."

Höfund stood now. "Reckon I could hold it steady enough while you climb. Long as you're going one at a time, leastwise."

Meaning the half-jotunn would be left behind on the rooftop. There were few people Hervor would rather have at her side if they ran into guards up there, but she had no better suggestion. She clapped him on the back and he nodded at her. Then he took the line from Vebiorg, wrapped it around his meaty forearm, and pulled it taut, with his feet braced against the lip of the roof.

Starkad eased himself onto that lip, grabbed the line with both hands, and then wrapped his legs around it too. Hand over hand, he pulled himself along. He made progress quickly, though a sheen of sweat had risen on Höfund's brow before Starkad reached the balcony.

"I'll go next," Hervor said. She shouldn't have let Starkad go first. The man could barely see anymore.

She climbed onto the lip and repeated Starkad's tactic, edging her way up along the rope. Halfway through, her hands were burning. Cold sweat tickled down her neck. Pulling herself along with naught but the strength of her arms left her panting. And wondering if all the others could even pull this off.

The skin on her palms chafed from the rope. Come on. She could do this. She'd made harder climbs before. On several godsdamned occasions, in fact.

Grunting with the effort, she reached the balcony. The question was, how was she supposed to reach around behind herself and hold it? Awkward maneuver, even were she not dangling eighty feet above a cobbled road. If she fell from here, they'd be hard pressed to gather enough of her for a proper pyre.

"Hervor," Starkad whispered. "Take my hand."

There he was, arm outstretched over the rail. Hervor twisted around as best she could and lunged for his arm with her left hand. The motion jostled the line despite Höfund's obvious efforts. Her fingers brushed over Starkad's palm. Missed. Before she could even curse, his hand had wrapped around her wrist. She had to turn a bit to grasp his hand.

"Ready?" he asked.

Odin's stones. This was not going to be pleasant. Naught to do but get it over with, though. She released the line and lunged at the wall. Her half-useless right hand caught the rail. For a heartbeat.

Then she slipped, pitched over the side.

Starkad grunted, yanked forward. Her movement jerked to a sudden stop, slamming her hip against the side of the tower and threatening to tear her shoulder right out of its socket. Hervor clenched her teeth and stifled her gasp of pain.

"Get ... up ..." Starkad had both hands on her arm now.

Sucking in rapid breaths, she twisted around and caught his other arm with her right hand. Like that, she managed to edge her feet against the tower wall. He pulled slowly, letting her walk up the side several paces, until her foot brushed the bottom of the balcony. Then he heaved her up over the rail.

She collapsed on top of him and they both fell, panting. How in Hel's frozen underworld had he managed to get over that himself? Two working hands, she had to guess.

Starkad eased her off him, rose, and beckoned the others. Vebiorg made the climb faster and with more grace than either of them had. The varulf twisted around, grabbed the edge, and heaved herself up like it was naught at all.

It left Hervor shaking her head.

Vebiorg winked at her. Of *course* the varulf had seen Hervor's blunder earlier.

Tveggi followed, then Win. Then Afrid, and finally Baruch and Fjolvor.

Across the gap, she saw Höfund slump down.

Exhausted, no doubt, and he'd have to support them all once again on the way back down.

Once everyone was up top, Starkad began to circle around the balcony. Hervor chased close on his heels. Shortly, they came to an archway that led inside, through the thick outer wall and onto a landing. From this, a stairwell circled downward, leading deeper into the tower.

Tanna's office was in the upper reaches, so probably only one or two flights down from here. With a bit of luck, they'd be in and out of this place quick.

Starkad nodded at her, then started for the stairs.

Hervor grabbed his arm and leaned in close. "Let Vebiorg go first," she whispered. He glowered. "You can't see out of one eye. We need someone watching for guards who'll spot them before they see us. You know it's true."

Grumbling under his breath, he motioned the varulf forward, but started off right after her. That was fine. He could still fight, but Hervor wasn't about to let him get himself killed over his pride.

She crept on after him.

The stairwell wrapped around, with a let off at a small landing. Starkad and Vebiorg had paused before reaching it, staring at something. Peering over his shoulder, she caught a glimpse of a pair of guards down there.

Couldn't clearly make out what they had on them. Polerarms, maybe, though probably not at the ready.

Her crew would need to move fast, to silence those men before they could raise a shout. Starkad looked to Vebiorg. The two of them seemed to be thinking the same thing. He motioned for Hervor to fall back a step.

She did so. It was a tiny landing, and too many people would just get in the way.

He eased his swords free, then nodded at Vebiorg. The

woman took off with the speed of a real wolf. Starkad chased after her.

A quick yelp of surprise escaped one of the guards. The sound cut off soundly, muffled.

Hervor stepped down the stairs to find Vebiorg had slapped a hand over each guard's mouth and then driven their heads into the wall. An instant later, Starkad cut their throats. The two men collapsed, gurgling.

Well, that pretty well solved that. Hervor scrambled down to the landing, then motioned the others behind her to follow. There was only one door here, though the stairs continued down. But the two guards had flanked the door, so something good had to be beyond. Tanna's bedchamber if they were lucky.

Things were going well enough for now.

Vebiorg looked at everyone, then tried the door. The handle clicked, but wouldn't open.

"It's locked," Baruch whispered.

Oh. Well, that had seemed too easy, hadn't it?

Fjolvor set to searching the guards while Baruch knelt and examined a tiny hole in the door.

"I might be able to pick it," Baruch said, drawing a metal pin from inside his shirt.

"Won't it be barred from the other side, then?" Afrid asked.

"Not how they do it here," Baruch mumbled without looking away from the hole. He was fiddling with it, taking far too long. Every moment they wasted with this increased the chance someone would come along and find eight intruders and two dead guards.

She glanced at Starkad who was twitching one of his swords ever so slightly from side to side. Nervous? Him?

Vebiorg sniffed, staring at the stairs. "Whole tower reeks of blood. Lot of people died in here."

"And I don't want to be among them," Afrid said. "Would it be too much trouble to do this faster, Miklagardian?"

"Not helping," Baruch mumbled. A faint click sounded inside the door. "There." He rose and eased open the door.

What lay beyond was no bedchamber.

Instead, a half dozen chests of gleaming gold and silver coins glittered around the room, catching the firelight from the brazier out here. Piles of gems on a low table sparkled. Jewel-encrusted sword sheaths hung on a rack on the wall. All of it a hoard of wealth unlike aught Hervor had ever beheld nor even dreamed of.

Afrid blew out a whistle and pushed her way inside, immediately grabbing handfuls of the gems.

It broke Hervor out of her daze, and she joined the younger shieldmaiden. This might not have been why they'd come, but with so much wealth, Hervor could easily reverse Grandfather's fortunes. Could buy an army and ensure he gained a jarldom somewhere, if not the one he'd once held.

"We have little time for this," Win said. "We came here to accomplish a mission, not rob Lord Tanna."

Starkad was shoving silver coins in a pouch too. "We're not all princes here."

The others joined in, jamming whatever they could carry into bags and pouches and inside shirts. Even Tveggi had snatched one of the jeweled swords from the rack.

A Miklagardian shout went up out on the landing.

Hervor spun, hand on Tyrfing. A group of guards was flooding into the treasure room.

## 6

Starkad tore through the guards, whipping his blades around in rapid arcs. He twisted around, cut a man's throat and parried the halberd thrust of another. Behind him, the others were fighting too, but he couldn't keep track of them. He could barely mind himself now. Always had to keep turning to ensure no one could come up on his blind side.

Another guard fell at his feet as Starkad's blade cleaved through his chin. Blood splattered everywhere.

Screaming. The clank of metal on metal. The stench of shit and blood.

The utter chaos that accompanies any battle.

Hervor bellowed a war cry and slashed through a man's arm, Tyrfing barely slowing before it embedded in the poor bastard's chest.

Starkad whipped both blades together and rushed a man blocking the doorway. The guard caught the edge of a sword under his throat and fell back gurgling as Starkad pushed onward. With a growl, he shoved the man backward, sending the dying guard tumbling down the stairs.

Vebiorg leapt past him, caught a guard by the throat, and bodily hurled him into the far wall. The guard cracked his skull against the stone, hit the floor, and lay still.

"We still need to find the runeblade," Win shouted from somewhere behind them.

Fighting every warrior in Miklagard had not been part of the plan though. Maybe Starkad should send the others back up to the balcony, try to cover their retreat.

More warriors came tromping up the stairs, two of them, followed by a man in an ornate, blood-red robe with golden embroidery. At his hip rested a sheathed sword in a scabbard even more elaborately decorated than those in the treasure vault.

Tanna.

Starkad point his sword at the man. "Kill him!" He charged forward, but was intercepted by another two guards and had to dodge a halberd thrust.

Vebiorg dashed around him, lunged between the two guards—embedding her axe in one's skull—and grabbed Tanna's throat. Or tried to. The Patriarch moved even faster than the varulf, caught her wrist and spun. His momentum inexplicably hefted her aloft and he swung her down like her arm was the shaft of a pendulum. The man brought the varulf crashing straight into the floor. The sound of bones cracking reached Starkad, even over the tumult behind him.

He faltered a step and almost took a halberd blade to the face. Only Tveggi's sudden shove got him out of the way. Rollaugr's thegn roared, blade flashing as he charged Tanna. The Patriarch stepped around Tveggi like the man was moving through quicksand. He appeared almost out of nowhere, with a hand grasping the back of Tveggi's skull.

Tveggi flailed, trying to escape the man's grasp but somehow unable to break free.

Starkad gaped, uncertain what he was even seeing.

Tanna jerked his hand down, pulling Tveggi to his knees. The old thegn was screaming, clutching his head. Tanna placed his other hand on the man's forehead. Oh, fuck.

Starkad roared, charging in.

The Patriarch pushed his hands together. Tveggi's skull exploded into fragments of bone and brains and gore, coating Starkad's chest as well as everything around him.

Bellowing, Starkad launched lightning-fast slash after slash.

Tanna dodged around them as though they were dancing. A half dozen times Starkad's blades passed within a hair of the Patriarch. But they never found flesh.

Starkad had always believed the fastest man was the only one who mattered. And he'd always been the fastest man. But Tanna moved with ... inhuman speed and strength.

The lord grinned ever so slightly, exposing elongated upper canine teeth. A hint of red light gleamed in his eyes. Draug? He didn't look rotten.

"Tveggi," Win was moaning.

"Run!" Hervor bellowed. "Retreat."

Damn it! Starkad swung again, pivoted, and thrust his other sword up at the same angle he expected Tanna to dodge the first. His second blade just managed to scrape the lord's side. Tanna's sneer dropped in an instant, and he backed away, hand to his ribs. He lifted it up. Dark red blood dripped between his pale fingers.

"Not so smug now," Starkad said. Maybe the man could understand Northern. Maybe not. Didn't really matter.

In a single move, almost too fast to see, Tanna jerked his sword free. Faint purple light gleamed from runes running up the length of the blade. The man bared his teeth, exposing those ... fangs.

All right then.

Starkad lunged forward.

Tanna broke up into a cloud of dust. It billowed past Starkad, flowed around him like he was not even there. He spun to see the cloud reform into a man behind him.

Hervor was leading the others back up the tower, back toward the balcony.

Giving up.

Tanna's runeblade flashed, cleaving through both of Fjolvor's legs as she tried to run up the stairs.

The woman shrieked, pitched over backward, and toppled back onto the landing. The sheer suddenness of it left Starkad breathless, dimly aware of Baruch rushing to where his wife had fallen. Screaming in wordless, mad defiance.

Fjolvor convulsing as the shock set in.

Afrid was against the wall, spear trembling in her grasp, mumbling. Standing in a pool of her own piss.

Vebiorg struggling to rise with Hel knew how many broken bones.

Fuck. Fuck. Fuck.

Starkad sucked in a deep breath, willed his mind to calm. He lunged at Tanna, whipped his swords both around in a deadly dance. He had to save them. The ones he could. He'd brought them here, now he had to save them.

Tanna twisted around, broke into dust, and solidified beside Starkad, swinging. It took all Starkad had to twist out of the way, parrying. Tanna's runeblade came down again, shearing cleanly through one of Starkad's swords.

Win was dragging Baruch away from Fjolvor. If she wasn't dead yet, she soon would be.

Starkad flung the hilt of his broken sword at Tanna then took off running for the stairs himself, not waiting to see if the throw hit.

He dared a glance over his shoulder to see Vebiorg doffing her clothes, grunting in pain, and trying to climb the stairs all at once.

Tanna wasn't pursuing, though. He'd paused to lift Fjolvor up by the neck. The woman was mercifully unconscious. The ... creature bit into her neck and held her there, the both of them trembling.

What the fuck?

"Move!" Starkad bellowed at the others.

Vebiorg had become a wolf and was running. She dashed around him, leaving him the last one out. Starkad ran up to the balcony.

The clomping footfalls of guards chased him.

Afrid was already climbing the rope back to the other rooftop. But they'd never all make it.

How far down was it? Thirty feet, assuming he cleared the gap and made it to the other roof?

Vebiorg either followed his gaze or else had the same idea, because the varulf backed up, dashed forward and took a flying leap. She landed easily onto the next roof, Höfund jolting so violently Afrid almost pitched off the rope.

"We have to jump it!" he shouted. "Go! Go!"

"We can't make that!" Win objected.

A guard rushed him. Starkad sidestepped his halberd thrust, caught the shaft, and tugged. The man stumbled toward him, too close for Starkad to use his sword. So instead he jerked the cross guard up into the man's nose. It sent him tumbling down.

Beyond them, another robed man was closing in. His bared teeth revealed fangs like Tanna's.

"Hel's tits," Starkad said through gritted teeth.

Hervor screamed behind him. Must've made the jump. Please don't let her fall. He glanced back. She was on the other roof, laying on her side. Baruch was there too.

Just Starkad and Win still here.

The fanged man stepped up onto the wall and began walking along it toward Starkad, mouth wide. Oh, fuck this. Starkad spun, raced for the rail, and jumped. Let Win follow if he wasn't an imbecile.

Wind rushed past his face.

For a moment, he thought he'd fall short. But he crashed down just over the building's lip, rolled with it, and still slammed hard enough into the ground to knock his breath away.

As he rolled over, he saw Win try the jump. He didn't make it nigh as far, but Höfund released the grapple line and lunged out, catching the prince's wrist and heaving him on the building.

"What happened?" Höfund asked. "Did you kill Tanna?"

"No!" Hervor said, seeming hard pressed to gain her feet. "Now fucking run."

Shouts were up all over the area.

Some of the guards had climbed up on the rail to try the jump themselves.

Starkad scrambled to his own feet and dashed forward. The others were racing toward the next rooftop. It was one of those long ones, stretching out along the river, but angled.

Not ideal for jumping onto. Not that anyone of them had the least choice in the matter. Starkad raced for it, cleared the gap, and landed on the incline. His boots skidded a foot or so before he caught himself with one hand. Pushing off the tiles, he took off running again.

Hervor and Win were just ahead of him. No sign of Vebiorg, Baruch, or Afrid.

He glanced back. The other fanged abomination effortlessly made the jump from the balcony, landed in a crouch, and advanced on without hesitation.

Damn it!

Starkad raced forward, looking for the next rooftop. They had to lose that thing somehow.

Had to stay ahead of it.

Because Tanna had torn through his crew like a butcher.

7

*H*ervor jumped to another rooftop, landed wrong, and slid. Her knee cracked down on a shingle, dislodged the tile and sent it crashing down.

Win yanked her up by the elbow. "This way!" He was pointing around the bend created by a second tier on the current roof. No time to argue, really.

Hervor let the prince guide her. Win dashed around the bend, then scrambled off at an angle away from the river. Hervor was too fucking turned about to be sure, but she thought this route was taking them farther from the apartment where she needed to meet the others.

Hardly mattered, though. Anywhere was better than here.

Win leapt to another building, slightly lower than this one, landed in a crouch, and dashed forward.

Panting, Hervor chased after the prince. Odin's gods-damned stones. She *knew* coming to this city had been a mistake. What the hideous blood-drinking *fuck* were those things? Like draugar, almost, but Tanna had looked human.

Win scurried over the next rooftop, dislodging a hail of

tiles that came crashing onto the cobbled street below. No one down there to get hurt, but the noise of it seemed like to attract—

Dust billowed up before Win in a cloud bigger than he was. A red gleam rose up in that cloud, and then the cloud congealed into a man. Another fanged monstrosity.

Win turned so quick he toppled over sideways, rolled off the roof, and pitched down into the street below.

Troll shit!

Hervor twisted, looked down. A merchant stall stood just below her. With a glance at their attacker—now striding straight for her—Hervor leapt off. Landed on the stall's roof. The thin wood cracked under her feet. A single heartbeat, then she plunged through. Splinters scraped her arms and face as she dropped down into the ruined stall.

The second fall knocked the breath out of her. Everything was hazy for a moment. Groaning, Hervor scrambled out to the street and caught a glimpse of Win disappearing into an alley. Off-balance, she blundered after the man, hit her shoulder on the narrow alley wall, bounced off it, and kept running.

A hand lurched out from a tiny space between two buildings, grabbed her, and jerked her inside. She was wedged in so tight she could hardly move. But Win was still squeezing through.

Hervor's heart was beating all out of control. Over her shoulder, Tyrfing caught on the wall, scraping, making too damn much noise. She tried to reach for the hilt, but couldn't get her arm up. No choice but onward.

This narrow passage let out into another alley. Hervor had not the merest clue where they were. Whole place was a fucking maze.

Win was already darting down another narrow passage,

running blind, Hervor had no doubt. But she didn't have a better plan. Who knew how close that thing was?

She chased after Win. This passage opened back out into another market street. Shit, maybe the same one, who knew?

Win glanced around, then back over his shoulder. "Aesir preserve us."

The prince took off across the street, forcing Hervor to follow. He wasn't paying enough attention, had let fear take him.

There was a figure in the street, a man in a cloak, so not the same creature. One of Tanna's other men, maybe. And turning their way.

Hervor grabbed Win from behind and threw the both of them rolling into another merchant stall. She slapped a hand over Win's mouth and pulled him in close.

The man in the street looked around as if he'd heard them. Turned in their direction. His eyes gleamed red. His face was rotting. But she knew it. Orvar-Oddr.

Of all the godsdamn bad timing possible ... Why now? Odin's bulging stones, why *now*? How did the bastard even know she was in Miklagard?

Win wriggled, had maybe suddenly realized he was looking at a draug.

Hervor pulled him tighter, low, so they could hardly even see out the edge of the stall. If Orvar hadn't seen them yet, maybe ...

The draug stalked closer. Looked about. Passed so nigh Hervor could smell the stench of decay off him.

She clenched her own teeth to keep them from chattering. Willed her wild heartbeat under control. Couldn't let him find her. Not now. Maybe he'd kill her, maybe not. He'd sure as Hel kill Win, though, and probably torture Hervor.

All she had to do to end this was kill him, though. Just draw Tyrfing, close the distance, and stab him in the back. She'd done it when he was alive. Except now, he was stronger and faster than ever.

And she couldn't make her treacherous hand release Win to grab the sword. She was holding on to him to steady herself as much as to keep Win still.

Every time she'd tried to fight the Arrow's Point, he'd hurt her. Years of it. She couldn't beat him. He was too strong. If Höfund was here …

With a start, Hervor realized it wasn't Win trembling in her arms, it was herself.

Because Orvar had turned her craven.

§

"I-I think this is the way," Win mumbled for the third time. He'd been muttering under his breath about Tveggi from almost the moment they'd left that merchant's stall.

By all rights, Hervor should have been the one leading them back to the apartment. Starkad had more or less declared her his second, true. But right now, Hervor just couldn't quite make her brain work, much less her body or heart.

Dumbly, she followed behind Win. All this felt like some waking nightmare. She could only assume Tanna and his men were some new kind of draugar. As if Hervor had not had enough of the deathless abominations on Thule and in the years following it.

On that cursed ship she had somehow sailed into the Otherworlds and never, ever, been able to pull free of them. They had their grasp on her and would not let go.

"There," Win said. "I definitely recognize those stalls."

"How can you even tell with all the goods removed?"

"Trust me."

Hervor shrugged. Maybe the prince did know some-thing. Either way, it seemed as good a course as any. She followed him until, indeed, the back alleys did start to look familiar, if more eerie in the night and deserted of all life.

Deserted ... Everyone fled the streets before nightfall here. Because they *knew*. Even if they didn't know exactly what prowled the night, they knew something did. And Baruch was from this city. Even as a child, shouldn't he have known?

Win took a wrong turn, and they had to double back before they came to the apartment Baruch had rented for them. The door was shut, but voices sounded within. Hervor eased open the door.

Starkad had his hands on the hilts of his swords at her intrusion. "Hervor. I feared ..." He shook himself.

Hervor stepped inside, followed by Win. Höfund was there, and Afrid, huddling in a corner and trembling, arms wrapped around her knees. Beside her sat Vebiorg, with a blanket wrapped around her waist and another draped over her shoulders. No spare clothes?

"Where's Baruch?" Hervor asked.

"We're not sure," Starkad said. "Maybe he didn't make it. There were soldiers all over the city. And more of those crea-tures stalking us."

Hervor grimaced. "He's the only one who knows aught about this cursed place. Without him—"

"Tanna has the runeblade, Mistilteinn," Starkad said. "It's the last of them still lost to the North Realms. We have to claim that."

"And kill Tanna," Win said. "As long as he lives—"

"Lives?" Afrid asked. "He seemed to me more like a draug."

"Indeed," Win said, "but do not interrupt me again. Of all the shocking things, we saw an actual draug on the streets. One of Tanna's minions, no doubt, assuming the locals don't keep the things as pets. Through the grace of Odin alone, he didn't see us."

Starkad frowned. What was he thinking? He couldn't know aught about Orvar-Oddr ... He couldn't. "I had reason to believe some ancient, fell powers lurked in the city, though I didn't know—"

"Someone's coming," Vebiorg said. She sniffed the air. "Baruch."

"Odin be praised," Win mumbled. "We've lost enough people already. We lost ..."

Everyone fell silent.

Tveggi had trained Win, hadn't he? Like Gunther had taught Hervor, except the prince seemed to have appreciated the man even before he was dead. Loved him, the way she ought to have loved her tutor with the sword. But then, Hervor had always been an ungrateful bitch. And now it was too late to make it up to Gunther or anyone else. All she had left was Grandfather and Starkad.

Hervor wished she had aught to say that might comfort Win. She'd lost enough friends to know naught would.

Baruch flung open the door. "They've found us."

Vebiorg growled, already on her feet and stalking out the door, axe in hand.

"Gods damn it," Afrid said. "They really ought to warn travelers in the harbor about this place. Enter at your own risk. The locals will kill and eat you."

"Everyone up," Starkad snapped. "Move."

How the fuck had they found them so quickly? What was going on in this city?

Baruch beckoned everyone onward, waving as the crew piled out of the apartment one by one. "This way. There's a grate to the sewers down the alley."

"What are sewers?" Hervor asked.

"You don't want to know," Baruch said. "Just move." He led them scrambling down the next alley. Vebiorg dashed past him. "Wait!" he called. The man paused at a metal grate in the middle of the ground. Knelt and grabbed it, clearly straining to heft it up.

Höfund grabbed hold of it, yanked it up, then wrinkled his nose. "Smells like rank shit down there."

"Accurate enough," Baruch said. "Jump in."

"Sure," said Afrid. "But how about you tell us your real plan."

Baruch shook his head and slid down the circular hole, landing below with a slight splash.

Hervor glanced at Starkad.

"Do it," he snapped. "All of you."

Afrid grimaced. "No, really. I think it's probably filthy down there. I'd like to request a new option."

Hervor slid down onto her arse and let her legs dangle. "Your other option is getting eaten." Then she dropped down into the dark tunnel beneath.

She landed in muck up to her ankles. The stench almost bowled her over.

Baruch was ahead, had already lit a torch. The tunnel itself was arched, with holes in the upper reaches every so often, from which dribbled more streams of filth.

Odin's stones. What possessed men to build this?

"The rain washes some of it down," Baruch said, as if she had actually asked. "Keeps the city above from drowning in

61

its own waste. Nicer homes have pits that drop directly in here."

"Pits?"

"Holes where people can shit down."

He was serious, wasn't he?

Behind her, she heard the others dropping down into these sewers.

"Keep moving," Starkad said. "With luck, they won't know we've come down here. It'll be hard for them to track us."

Hervor shook her head. Mist-madness had brought her here. And now, all she wanted was a way out.

## 8

Three Moons Ago

*T*he Yngling hall in Upsal sat on the edge of the Fyris Wood, uncomfortably close to marshland, really. Still, that same supposedly haunted forest had covered their approach. Her and Starkad and Lennius. Not Aun, of course. The Yngling lacked the stones to even come and watch the holmgang, much less fight it himself.

And now here they were, back in the hall of Hervor's former enemies.

Ole was a big man, sprawled over the throne like he couldn't be bothered to act royal. Maybe in his youth he'd been fit, but by now he'd earned a gut that bespoke too much mead. Still had arms that looked fit to snap a tree trunk in half, though.

The king had welcomed them warm enough, even offered them food from his table and mead to drink. Kind of made Starkad's purpose here sit even less well with Hervor. She sat at the table beside Lennius while Starkad bantered with the king he'd come here to murder.

All of it a sham.

"You've done well for yourself," Starkad said. "Urd favors you of late."

Ole chuckled. "Urd is a fickle bitch, as you well know. One day she's got her mouth around your cock, and the next you know, you're the one on your knees."

Hervor snorted at that. Poor bastard had no idea how right he was.

Starkad scratched at his beard. "Unfortunately, that's why I'm here."

Ole slapped a meaty palm on his armrest. "So! Urd been mistreating you, my friend?" The king inclined his head to where Lennius sat. "Not keeping the best of company, I see, though. Does make a man wonder at your purpose here."

Now Hervor's lover shrugged. "I rather think it makes the purpose obvious enough."

"Argh. Maybe it does, at that. But then, who's to say I shouldn't just have my men cut his head off and be done with it?"

Oh. That wasn't good. Because if Ole was going to have Lennius killed, it seemed more like than not he might try the same with her and Starkad. Hervor shifted just a little, making sure Tyrfing was in easy reach.

Starkad cast a wary glance at her and offered the barest shake of his head. Man knew what she was thinking. "You start murdering your guests, you're like to find yourself with fewer friends and more enemies."

The king scoffed. "Can't say that sounds much different than where I'm seeing myself now, friends turning against me."

"The difference is, I'm offering you a fair fight. One on one—a holmgang. The old way. You win, you keep your honor and everyone knows you bested Aun's champion."

Now Ole snorted. "And if I lose, I'm fucking dead. Can't say as that's overly tempting."

"You lose and maybe you see Valhalla. We both know you've got the stones to make it a good fight, one way or the other. But if you back down from the challenge ..."

"You're a right bastard, Eightarms. Trying to put me in a position like that."

Starkad nodded. "You're probably right. But did you really think you could come and take away a man's kingdom without it costing you aught? Especially if you were fool enough to let that king escape."

"You think I didn't try? Little shit-eater crawled behind Gylfi's skirts. Would you've had me march on Dalar too now? Couldn't have done. Not when that sorcerer was alive, leastwise."

Wait, what?

Starkad faltered. "Gylfi?"

Ole chuckled. "Oh, you didn't hear that already? Word came this very day he was murdered down in Skane, torn down by varulfur. Hardly clear what's happened, but some are blaming Siggeir Wolfsblood." Now the man lurched to his feet, his throne groaning as he did so. Standing, he was even more impressive. Practically a snow bear. "See, nobody makes war in winter. So for now, Aun is safe in Dalar, stewing in his own piss and trembling like a fucking trench. Come summer, maybe I'll take your advice and finish what I've started."

"Gylfi ... is truly dead?"

The big man shrugged, his gut jiggling with the motion. "Seems even sorcerers can't stave off death forever. It comes to us all, Eightarms. But you've the truth of it ... I can't rightly refuse your challenge without looking a craven before my own men. And we both know I'm no craven."

"We do indeed."

"Tomorrow, then. Not dawn. I wouldn't wake that early for Odin his godsdamned self. But in the morn, by the wood. And Eightarms? I'll see you get the funeral you deserve. A proper pyre and all that. Some of us remember old friendships. You faithless wretch."

❧

HERVOR STOOD on the edge of the holmgang circle. Most times, men preferred to do this the old way, on an island. Here, though, everyone was so eager to see it done, they'd just formed a ring of torches stuck in the snow, maybe fifteen feet across.

A tight space, truth be told.

Especially considering Ole the Strong seemed to take up half the damn circle himself with his bulk. The man beat an oversized axe against his shield, that too, larger than average.

Starkad circled around him, swords in hand, a wolf stalking a mammoth. Usually, Hervor would have counted that a stupid fucking wolf. Still, Starkad was light on his feet, limber next to Ole's plodding tromp. Starkad clanked his swords together in acknowledgement.

Ole roared, rumbling forward like an avalanche. Not fast. Not at first, but his momentum built with each passing foot.

Starkad leapt to the side and Ole plowed into a pair of men standing on the circle's edge. Sent them both sprawling in the snow.

Maybe Starkad could've lunged in and ended it right there, but he waited, allowed Ole to turn about and face him again. Too much honor to Hervor's mind. Or maybe he hesitated over an old friendship. Either way, it stood to cost him.

Ole lunged forward, swinging that axe in great arcs.

There was no parrying an attack like that. Starkad twisted out of the way, unable to close the distance. When Ole swung again, Starkad spun around, whipping his sword toward Ole's massive gut.

The big man moved faster than he had any right to and jerked his shield forward. The wooden circle caught Starkad's sword, kept going, and slammed into his chest. The blow lifted Hervor's lover bodily off his feet and flung him backward before he landed in the snow, gasping.

A heartbeat later and Ole was chopping down with that axe.

Hervor sucked in a sharp breath. Starkad rolled to the side, kicked his foot out, and caught Ole in the knee. The move stunned the larger man and he faltered, one leg giving out under him. Starkad rolled over backward and scrambled away.

Suddenly aware her hand was on Tyrfing's hilt, Hervor released it. She couldn't interfere. No one could. A holm-gang was a sacred duel. Didn't always have to be to the death, but this one was. It was the whole purpose of Starkad coming here.

The pair of them danced about. Or Starkad danced, narrowly avoiding vicious blow after vicious blow. Ole didn't seem concerned with skill or grace so much as raw power. And he had a lot of it. He ignored a half dozen scratches Starkad scored on his face, arms, and legs. Just kept blundering forward, getting more and more wild.

Now he was fuming, spittle flying from his mouth as his axe cleaved the air, whistling.

Before that mara had ravaged him, Starkad would've

ended this long ago. Now, Hervor wasn't so sure it was hesitation slowing him. Pain and fatigue, maybe. Plus not being able to see so well. This had been a stupid plan. Odin's stones, it was stupid. She should've killed Aun herself for even suggesting this.

Ole whipped his axe up in a rising arc. Starkad leapt to the side, narrowly avoiding being split from groin to skull. One of his blades came around and sliced into the side of Ole's throat. The blundering oaf staggered. He raised his axe-wielding hand to his neck then stared at the blood on his knuckles. More of it dribbled out of his mouth.

Starkad twisted around behind him, whipping his other blade around to cut out Ole's hamstring. The oaf roared in pain and pitched over into the snow.

Panting himself, Starkad stalked up behind him. Flipped his grip around on one of his swords. And drove it straight down through the back of the man's neck.

The whole crowd had fallen silent. Staring at Starkad in disbelief.

Hervor shut her own half-open mouth.

Starkad looked to her, then limped away from the bloody circle, one hand to his side.

Hervor caught his arm as he drew nigh and led him toward the wood. Maybe nobody would've dared interfere with the holmgang. It didn't mean none of those bastards Ole had brought from Reidgotaland wouldn't murder them in their sleep in revenge.

It was best the three of them were fast away from Upsal, at least until Aun managed to come back with no few warriors loyal to his dynasty.

"You're lucky to be alive you stupid fuck," she whispered to Starkad.

"I love you too."

"Don't change the godsdamned subject. Do you even care about Aun? I mean, really?"

"No."

"No, of course you don't." She spat. "No, someone just has to mention silver or gold and your cock is hard, isn't it? How many fortunes do you need to gain and lose, Starkad? When will it be enough?"

He shrugged off her shoulder. "Enough? I don't know. I can't ..."

Can't walk away. His godsdamned curse. And it had almost cost her him. Again.

"It's for you, anyway," he said.

"What?"

"The gold. You can use it to rebuild your home."

She scoffed. "It would help. Wouldn't have meant troll shit if you'd died, though. Besides, you think Hrethel will ever let Grandfather hold a title again? Some things can't be fixed."

Starkad groaned. "Gylfi."

"What?"

"There'll be a funeral."

Stood to reason. The oldest, most famed king in all Sviarland, maybe all the North Realms. There'd be a mighty funeral, probably held off as long as possible, just to give people from all the kingdoms time to attend. "You didn't even like him."

"Like him?" Starkad shook his head. "It was more complicated than that."

Everything always was with Starkad. Never a simple answer. Always another secret.

"I have to be there."

Fair enough. At the moment, Dalar was probably a far safer place for them than Upsal, anyway.

## 9

Starkad could not shake the sense of someone powerful pursuing them. An intuition, really, but since Wudga had awakened the Sight in him, he had to try to trust those instincts. Could their foes have realized they went into the sewers? Maybe they'd have checked the alley, seen that opened grate.

But these interconnecting tunnels were as much a maze as the city above, if not more so. And surely no one could track them through the waters down here. Even varulfur ought not to be able to follow their scents through this over-powering reek.

Yet he couldn't shake the feeling. That nameless dread roiling around in his gut. The sensation of continuous peril coming for him. For ... Hervor. And the others, too, now his responsibility.

He trudged forward, through the muck, to catch up to Baruch.

Odin's cryptic warnings had not prepared him for this. Maybe they should have, but the Ás either didn't know what they'd face here, or had chosen not to reveal it plainly. Who even knew what motivated Odin anymore? Manipulative bastard.

"I need to know what we're up against," he said to Baruch, keeping his voice low. Vebiorg would hear, no doubt. Damn varulfur had the ears of the wolves after all. But no sense in further terrifying the others until he had to. "You may have left this city as a child, but even at that age, you had to have known something was amiss here at night."

Baruch glanced back at the others. His torch cast his face in shadows, but still, Starkad could make out a clear grimace. "I remember ... hiding at night. It was just what we did. No one ever said why, but even orphans didn't go out after sunset. We'd squat anywhere we could, huddled together, waiting for dawn."

"I need more than that. What are those things?"

"I ... People tell ghost stories at night. In case we weren't frightened enough already. I remember a few. One tale, about the restless dead, they rise from the grave. They, uh ... sustain themselves on the living."

"Draugar."

"Um ..." Baruch kept looking back over his shoulder like he expected the creatures to sneak up on him if he even said it. "Maybe I thought so. I mean, draugar sometimes eat the flesh of the living, right? But these things, they could make you think they were human, at least some of them did. The story ... it was a long time ago. But it said, sometimes those who went out at night, you'd find their bodies, pale and cold, like something sucked the life out of them. That lord ... Fjolvor, he ..."

"I know."

"You think if I knew ... If I had any idea what would ..." Baruch shivered, looked ready to retch.

Tanna had paused in pursuing them to bite Fjolvor, who

would've died anyway. Bite her and seem to be drinking the blood of her wound.

Given the choice, Starkad would've left Baruch to grieve in peace. He didn't have that option, though. Not while Tanna and his minions were pursuing the rest of them.

"So the creatures in your stories?" Starkad asked.

"Vampires. That's what they were called."

"How do we kill them?"

"I don't know. I was a godsdamned child, Eightarms. I haven't thought of those stories in decades. And now my *wife* is dead."

Starkad grabbed him by his left arm and jerked him to a stop. "I sympathize. I do. Truly. But we will all be dead if we cannot figure out how to fight back against these foes."

"How do you kill a draug?" Baruch asked.

By now the others had caught up, were watching the conversation.

"You can burn it with fire. Or cut its head off."

Afrid snorted. "Hardly makes them special. You encounter aught that setting it on fire and cutting its head off *won't* kill? If so, that's a place I want to visit even less than this one."

Hervor groaned. "Cutting the head off something that godsdamned fast wouldn't be easy."

No, it wouldn't. But they were going to have to try. "Keep moving." He turned and pressed on.

The tunnel led into a domed chamber, with the center of it at a higher elevation, out of the muck. The crew all climbed up onto this, Afrid mumbling under her breath while kicking her boots like she could shake the filth off them. Or like she wouldn't have to hop back in it to leave here. Five other tunnels exited this circular chamber, all but one of them low enough the muck flowed through them as well.

More interesting, though, the walls of the chamber were decorated with thousands upon thousands of multicolored stones. Layers of grime covered them, especially nigh to the water, but they seemed to be depicting a picture.

Instead of joining the others on the platform, Starkad grabbed a torch and walked closer to the wall. It was hard to tell where the picture began, but it seemed to be showing another city, one with spiked spires beneath a dark night sky.

In this city, numerous factions seemed to be held at uneasy peace. Factions of vampires?

*Ancient bloodlines ...*

It was almost a voice in his head. A memory of a dream, maybe. A warning Odin had tried to give him in his sleep, and one he'd forgotten.

This looked like twelve of these factions. Twelve bloodlines.

*Waiting for the changing of the world ...*

These creatures were ancient, from long before the Old Kingdoms. Before the mists, even, maybe. Naught like the city Starkad saw here existed on Midgard, at least not so far as he'd seen. In Utgard, perhaps, but maybe whatever this was had instead fallen into ruin long ago. Become naught but dust.

While still the vampires endured.

*Sleeping away in the ages ... Dead and deathless ...*

The picture continued, depicting what Starkad could only assume was the founding of the city by this very river. The founding of it by these ancient vampires. Wakened, somehow.

Miklagard had survived the mists, flourished where

most of mankind faltered and dwindled. Because Other-worldly powers led them. Like the Serklanders who worshiped Fire vaettir, except these creatures might not be possessed by vaettir so much as tied to the ghost world. Living ghosts themselves, maybe.

"What are you doing over there?" Hervor called.

Starkad glanced back at the others. "I think ... it's not just Tanna. All the Patriarchs, even the emperor himself. They are immortals. These vampires."

"Not possible," Baruch said. "No. That cannot be. These were just stories ..."

Starkad continued around the circle as it depicted the construction of the great towers of Miklagard. Rising as the empire rose. And finally, they fell into conflict with men whose hands were engulfed in flame: the Serklanders.

So what did it mean? That Miklagard's wars with Serk-land were all that held the vampire lords back from expanding their reach? But Serkland was being hard-pressed by the Vallanders since they'd allied with the Aesir. Maybe the other empire had begun to redirect its forces to the front at Andalus. Leaving the Miklagardians freer to press into Bjarmaland. Toward Holmgard.

So ... Did they put these creatures in charge of every place they conquered? If they took Holmgard, if they enthroned a vampire king to rule it, they could use that as a staging ground to reach Sviarland or Kvenland. To flood their kind into all the North Realms.

Starkad swallowed, looked back at Hervor. They weren't really paying attention. Didn't realize what all this meant. And if they had, it might well have broken them. Most people couldn't handle the truth that their world was so very fragile. That at any moment, it might collapse, beset by horrors on all sides.

And if their mission here failed, if they didn't stop Tanna's advance on Holmgard, they had more to lose than a single small kingdom.

Meaning, no matter what it took, Starkad would kill Tanna and claim Mistilteinn. These Miklagardian vampires would learn what men of the North Realms had in them.

## 10

*L*ong years of travels had brought Orvar to Miklagard once before, when fighting pirates on the Black Sea alongside his son. Another lifetime, really, and like the memories of his life, it was dimmed and distant, tainted by the red haze of fury that so consumed his every thought.

*Vengeance. Vengeance. Vengeance.*

For the world had failed him. For all he had known once, long ago, mattered naught.

*Vengeance.*

It coiled around his mind like a linnorm, venom-laced fangs sunken deep into his brain.

*Vengeance.*

Upon Hervor, first and most of all. Murderer. Murderer.

And she had dared to come here, even knowing he had picked away at those nigh to her one by one. Craven, perhaps, she had fled and left her Grandfather to his urd. As the old man wilted and withered, perhaps Hervor even hoped Orvar would put an end to him and spare her the pain of doing it herself.

He strode down the empty streets toward the tower rising up ahead of him. An impressive construction. One that had—in life—filled him with awe and inexplicable disquiet. Now, it almost beckoned.

Naught else of the deaths around Hervor seemed to have fazed her. For she had so little soul left in her, perhaps, and cared naught for any save herself. And Starkad Eightarms.

Hard to believe they had become lovers. Hard to believe she had love in her at all.

Fitting, then, that the last thing Orvar would take from her before ending her was Starkad.

*Vengeance. Vengeance. Vengeance.*

Long had he waited for its fulfillment. So long peering through the haze of red, waiting for her to break. Too long, for she was already a pathetic, heartless wretch before he had begun. Too long, and now he was done with her.

Vengeance, long awaited, and its time had come at last. And so Orvar would rip the beating heart from Hervor's chest and bite deep into it, devour it whole and be sated. At least for a moment.

And dare to believe, to hope, that might abate the pain that wracked him.

For the deathless spend every moment trapped in the agony of dying.

Stone steps led up to the single doorway in the tower, the door made of steel—not iron, of course—with banded strips across it. Shut tight, though few in this city would dare approach in any event. Nachzehrer, some had called these creatures in the North Realms, those few who did not mistake them for draugar. And perhaps they were related, but not quite the same.

Orvar rapped hard upon the steel door.

It creaked open a moment later, and red pinpricks of

eyes greeted him from the darkness beyond. Darkness and a hint of dust in the air, disturbed despite a lack of airflow.

"I am the Arrow's Point," he said. His Miklagardian was not good, but good enough. "Come to seek an audience with the Patriarch."

The eyes winked out and the door creaked open further, inviting him into the darkness.

Orvar stepped inside, into a small landing beneath a stairwell.

An iron-like grip snatched his elbow and pulled him deeper inside.

The door slammed shut, leaving him in nigh to total darkness. But then, like any other creature of the darkness, he needed little light with which to see.

His own eyes would no doubt have shone with red light as he turned toward the vampire holding his arm.

The creature flinched, ever so slightly, clearly unaccustomed to seeing aught else of the Otherworlds walking in its city. "Move." Its voice a whisper, hardly the rasping hollow thing Orvar's own voice had become.

Did vampires not fall prey to the rot of the grave? Or did they merely have a way to disguise its ravages?

Such questions mattered little, in truth.

Only one thing mattered.

*Vengeance.*

The drum, beating in his head, throbbing where his pulse ought to have been. A rhythm pounded out against his skull.

*Vengeance. Vengeance. Vengeance.*

The vampire guided him up the stairs, several flights of them, until they must have reached close to the top of the tower.

Nigh to seven years now he'd suffered the agonies of

death. Until the drumbeat had faded into the background enough he could—for brief moments—almost forget it was there. But it was never gone. Just as he would never live again.

*Vengeance.*

On a large landing, a man sat on a gold-embroidered couch resting upon a covered dais. Every speck of it bespoke opulence and grandeur and hubris on a scale that would've put an Ás to shame. The dais's overhang glittered in the light from the braziers set nearby, the sides of it seeming plated with actual gold, and that engraved with elaborate designs.

The walls were painted with equally intricate composi- tions, from flowing scripts to flowery red and gold patterns. Alabaster columns supported a small balcony that looked down on this landing from a higher floor on the tower.

On this couch lounged a man in an elegant crimson robe, seeming every bit the statesman, save for the crusting of dried blood over his chin and upper lip and, yes, even partway down his neck.

"I cannot recall being sought out by one of your corrupted kind before," Tanna said.

Orvar shrugged off the vampire escort, who released him. "Am I so much more corrupt than the aristocracy of Miklagard?"

Tanna quirked a slight smile, exposing a hint of fang. "I was speaking more of your putrefying flesh than the subtle, labyrinthine politics of the empire. Admittedly, millennia of internecine struggles have created a game that would appear hopelessly impenetrable to an outsider. I cannot say that the bemusement of foreigners much concerns us, though."

Orvar struggled to untangle the vampire's words which

rather strained his mastery of the language. "I did not come here to exchange witticisms," he finally said in Northern.

Tanna frowned now, as if the sound of the words was distasteful to him. "No. Your kind are like wraiths," he answered in Northern. "Driven by single-minded obsessions. No revenant could have built or even envisaged a society such as we have created here."

No doubt true. It became hard to think on aught else while that drum continued beating.

*Vengeance. Vengeance. Vengeance.*

"Perhaps not. But strange circumstances may have aligned our interests."

Tanna cocked his head to the side but said naught.

"The foe I seek not only came to your city, but broke into your tower. Her mission to kill you may have been ill-advised. But given that she did try, perhaps you too might be motivated ... by a desire for revenge."

"Why would I need your help? I have a small army of vampires hunting them even now. The blood of one of the intruders already helped me find their lair. They run low on places to hide."

Orvar frowned. He hadn't known these vampires could do that. "Like you, she bears a runeblade."

That got Tanna leaning forward.

"I know her. I know of her companions. Working together, we can hunt them and kill them, with less risk to yourself or your ... progeny."

Tanna's mirthless smile had returned. "Very well, revenant. Prove your worth and I will forestall my distaste for your kind. Tell me about these foreign interlopers. Tell me everything."

## 11

Starkad led their crew down the dry tunnel. They'd passed a few more grates that led back to the upper city, but until daylight broke, it seemed safer down here. Much as Hervor misliked these foul tunnels, at least naught was trying to drink her blood here.

Along the walls, more of those pictures—Baruch called them mosaics—decorated the tunnels.

Many sections of them were cracked or even turned to dust entirely, exposing crumbling wall beneath them. Other parts were so faded or filthy she couldn't guess at what they depicted.

Starkad had told her he suspected these tunnels represented some sort of history of the vampire bloodlines. From what he could make of them, there might once have been twelve bloodlines. Perhaps one for each of the Patriarchs? That would make sense. The emperor must've appointed the highest ranking member of each line as a lord of the empire.

Hervor had begun studying the mosaics herself at that. They depicted plenty of men and women who might've

81

been vampires, but none she'd clearly call the emperor. As to who or what that emperor himself was—assuming he existed—Hervor had no idea.

No clear indication in any mosaic. "Suppose he's a lie?" she asked Starkad, when he paused beside her to inspect another picture. "Suppose the Patriarchs tell the people they report to someone, some shadowy figure. Just to keep them united, keep them in line?"

"Could be. Doesn't matter overmuch though. This only reinforces that we need to kill Tanna."

Obsessed with his mission? Right now, all Hervor wanted was to make it out of this city alive. She'd already filled her pouches with coin stolen from Tanna. She'd just as soon keep that and her life both. "I don't get you."

"These vampires' bloodlines have some kind of rough truce between them."

"And?"

"If the Patriarch of one bloodline died, it would throw the others into chaos, scrambling to fill the void. While they fight each other, they're not bothering with Holmgard."

Maybe. Hervor moved on, not eager to spend too long in one place. "You're assuming the others wouldn't band together to avenge Tanna."

"I don't get the impression they much love each other."

Hervor grunted. "Doesn't mean they'll be pleased to find foreign humans coming in and murdering one of their number."

Starkad faltered, glanced at her. "You might be right. We can hope otherwise, though."

He didn't get it. "How can you hope for *aught* after all we've seen? The world of men is fucking doomed, Starkad." She glanced up at the others to make sure they were out of earshot. "It's going to be trampled under by jotunnar. Or overrun by draugar. Or consumed in fire from the likes of Scyld and the Serklanders. Or devoured by the godsdamned svartalfar waiting beyond the Veil. And you didn't even see the horrors in Pohjola." She shook her head, finding a tremble welling up in her chest. Saying it all aloud ... she'd been thinking Midgard would fall for a while. But she hadn't really talked it over with him. "Maybe Odin can save us, maybe not. But naught we do is going to stop the end."

"You have no idea what Odin really is."

"Right, well, maybe don't let Win hear you talk that way. Either way, we have to focus on what *we* can get out of life while some little bit of it is left to us."

A low growl echoed from the tunnel up ahead, where the others had treaded.

Hervor exchanged a look with Starkad, then they both charged forward.

Three—no, four—of those vampires had surrounded the rest of the group. One had Vebiorg pinned against the wall, the two of them wrestling and snarling, both growling.

Höfund was circling another, big axe hefted up.

A third had Win by the back of the neck while Baruch faced off with it, clearly not daring to draw nigh.

The last was stalking around Afrid as she spun, trying to keep up with its erratic, shadowy movements.

Hervor jerked Tyrfing free of its sheath and charged at that last one, trusting Starkad to help Win. She didn't utter a sound, but the vampire turned at her sloshing footfalls, bared its fangs, and brought up its own short-bladed sword.

Snarling now, Hervor lunged, chopped. Hit naught but air as the vampire twisted away, nimble as a damn bee. It darted around her like it was really made of dust blowing on the wind, so fast she could barely keep him in view. Her foot caught on her own ankle trying to turn about so quickly.

Afrid lunged forward with a knife—she'd lost her spear on those rooftops. The vampire spun around, sidestepped, and cuffed her on the cheek. The blow actually hefted the shieldmaiden off her feet and sent her spinning around in the air before crashing down into the muck, sending a wave of it splashing over Hervor.

Hervor shrieked, cleaving with Tyrfing into the vampire. It twisted away again, but not quite fast enough, as the blade bit into its ribs. Could it poison that which did not live?

The creature howled in rage, hand to its side. Without warning it launched itself at her, sword whistling through the air.

Hervor jerked Tyrfing up to parry. The impact jolted her arms and drove her backward. Odin's stones, this thing was strong. It came around again, blade darting in toward her gut. She leapt aside, knocking the blade wide, though it still scraped against her mail.

Reversing that parry, Hervor swung up at the vampire's face. It bent backward with superhuman speed and she only caught the tip of its chin. Driving it into further frenzy.

One of the other vampires was shouting in Miklagardian. Somewhere close behind her. She didn't dare look, though. Take her eyes off this one for an instant and it was like to rend her apart.

It flew into attack after attack, seeming as fast as Starkad. Faster, maybe. Her arms were numb from parrying it. Sweat streamed down her neck. No way she could beat this thing. Maybe Starkad could. Maybe Höfund could match its strength. But a human like her ... All she could do was hold out and hope one of the others could get to her.

The vampire's blade gouged her thigh and sent Hervor stumbling backward, her leg threatening to give out underneath her. Falling in this muck with an open cut was like to lead to infection and slow, rotting death. Assuming the vampire didn't give her a fast, messy end first.

Something grabbed the back of her neck. And then she was sailing through the air, twisting round. Everything spinning. Chaos and whooshing air.

A smack against hard stone.

A fall. A splash.

Darkness.

## 12

Three Moons Ago

*O*ut over the river, the funeral ship blazed, carrying away Gylfi's corpse. Arms folded across her chest, Hervor watched the ship growing smaller and smaller. The sorcerer king had ruled Dalar for longer than she'd been alive. Much longer, in fact, if tales spoke true. He'd been the first to bring the North Realms word of the new gods.

Odin himself had come to Gylfi and told him of the rise of the Aesir and the fall of the Vanir. Hard to imagine, really. The Aesir had been her gods all her life. Odin this all-knowing, withered old man. Except Starkad claimed to have met him, too ... Either way, in her mind, when she tried to imagine the god, she saw someone much like Gylfi himself.

The sorcerer had saved her life with his Art. On the other hand, in doing so he'd subjected her to torments of the Otherworlds. Gotten her raped and tortured, even if it *might* have all been in her head. Naught good came from the Otherworlds, and for a man to dabble in the Art invited horrors.

It made it hard to grieve his passing. Besides, how did you let go of a figure like that, a man who'd been there forever? Holding Sviarland together, keeping the Seven Kings from destroying each other. Or maybe keeping any one of them from conquering all the land. No matter how she tried, she couldn't wrap her mind around him being gone.

And Starkad, he just stood on the riverbank, staring at the ship. Had hardly said a word in days. He'd had his own strange relationship to Gylfi and—like his connection to Odin—seemed loathe to explain in the least.

Maybe he stood only a few feet ahead of her. Felt like miles, though. Like she could never quite grasp him. Not now.

The new king, Svarflami—Gylfi's grandson—he led the crowd back into the hall. Starkad broke away and followed the king, brushed right past Hervor without a godsdamned word. Not even a nod.

Fuck him, then. If he wanted to wallow alone in his thoughts, she'd give him that. Let him do as he would. Instead of following the throng, Hervor stayed on the river-bank until the crowd had largely broken away.

She'd always stayed well clear of Svarflami in any event. He was the son of Gylfi's daughter Heithr and of Sigrlami, who Hervor's own grandfather had killed in Holmgard. Agantyr had taken Sigrlami's daughter, Eyfura, and Tyrfing too. Not that Svarflami could've known her kin had slain his father, but it felt foul mingling with him, knowing what Hervor knew.

And could Svarflami be the king his grandfather had been? Seemed nigh to impossible, really. So what would become of Sviarland now? Maybe Hrethel would claim it all. She'd caught sight of a few other kings here, Aun, even, but none she knew had the might or stones to stand up to Hrethel.

And Hrethel ... well, he deserved Hervor's wrath for what had befallen her *other* grandfather. Finding him like that, she'd been ready to swear a fresh oath of vengeance, save that Starkad had talked her down from it. That chafed worse than wearing mail with no padding, but ... But maybe she didn't have it left in her to uphold another oath of vengeance. She'd spent years working against the Ynglings, got many of them killed.

And what did it bring her?

Orvar-Oddr, stalking her with each passing moment. And she couldn't fucking stop him. Maybe Starkad could have, but Hervor couldn't let him ever find out she'd murdered his friend. One way or another, she'd have to find a way to kill the draug. She needed him burned to ash.

Sighing, she kicked up a pile of snow. Her world was well and truly fucked. Maybe ... maybe she needed help from someone else. Mercenaries, maybe. Aun owned them a hefty price in gold already.

And he'd gone inside, no doubt eager to affirm friendships with the other kings.

Shaking her head, Hervor trudged on after the others. Inside, Svarflami's hall was so thick with people she could hardly move without getting jostled about. That, and dozens of braziers billowing smoke up into the rafters. Everyone was milling about, trying to grab the drinking horn or find a seat on overcrowded benches. Trying to get a piece of the largest feast she'd ever seen.

A bunch of them had clustered around some brawl. Mix enough mead and enough people together, you'll get some scuffles. Slightly curious, she shouldered her way through the crowd. Only it was Starkad brawling. A big, red-haired man had him by his tunic, atop a table. The man flung Starkad along the length of the surface, spilling over platters and plates. Starkad slid right off the edge and hit the floor.

Hervor gaped. Odin's stones! She'd never seen another man beat Starkad. Was he still weakened from his ordeal?

She tried to shove her way through, but the crowd was too damn thick. A warrior and a shieldmaiden grabbed Starkad and hefted him up. He shook them off as the red-haired man approached. Starkad's hands edged toward his blades.

Shit.

Brawling was one thing. Turning this into a duel, that would serve no one. Hervor shoved forward, caught Starkad's eye and glowered.

He lowered his hands, glaring at the other man. "I came here to pay respects to a fallen king. Not to squabble with you, Odinson."

Odinson? Odin's ... Fuck. That was Thor? As in *Thor*?

Thor shrugged. "Should you reconsider ... I would relish a duel between us."

She knew her mouth hung open but she couldn't have shut it to stop a bird from flying in. Instead, she pushed forward, trying to get a better look at the Ás. Odin's actual son. Walking around and drinking and fighting.

Pummeling her lover.

Starkad grabbed her arm and yanked her away. She'd been reaching out to try to touch the god's arm, she realized. "Stay the fuck away from him."

"That was Thor ..."

Starkad scoffed. "Not you too. The man acts like a troll's arse and has the brains to match."

She flinched, looked around. If someone heard Starkad so disparage one of the Aesir, who knew what could happen? Worse than a brawl, she'd guess. "You have some quarrel with the Ás?"

He glowered, silent as usual, and pulled her along after him to the back of the hall. "Höfund is here," he finally said. "He was looking for you."

Hervor stumbled over her own feet. The noise of the crowd drowned out the sound of her groan. Barely. Höfund, who'd just asked Grandfather for Hervor's hand in marriage. Wonder how Starkad would react to that.

Bastard might even encourage it.

She couldn't rightly refuse to meet him, though. Not after all they'd been through together. Without him, maybe she'd never have been able to save Starkad from the mara. She'd sure never have made it out of Pohjola.

So she said naught as Starkad guided her to a bench where the half-jotunn sat. The man had a mouthful of some meat, grease dribbling down his face and sticking in his beard. He looked up as she approached, toothy grin just letting bits of food stick out. "Hervor!" Didn't even bother finishing chewing.

She blew out a breath, then clasped his forearm. "Höfund. Uh ... there's got to be a drinking horn around here." She glanced about, then motioned to a shieldmaiden holding it. The woman handed it over and Hervor took a long swig of the mead.

Höfund was loyal. A friend. Wouldn't do to insult him, even if she couldn't agree to wed him. He'd always helped her and ... Oh. Oh, Odin's glorious stones. Höfund was almost as strong as a draug. Maybe he'd be just the one she needed to help her hunt down and kill Orvar-Oddr without Starkad ever catching wind of it.

She handed the horn to Starkad, who himself drank long. "I thought you were in Holmgard?" she asked Höfund.

"Was. But I'd already come round here looking for you. Caught word of this gathering and figured as you'd be here. You ain't the easiest person to find, most times, what with the wandering around and so forth."

Damn it. He'd come to press his request for her hand, hadn't he? Last thing she needed was him raising it in front of Starkad. That'd be almost as troubling as having to discuss it alone with him.

"Got tired of Bjarmaland?" Starkad asked.

"Can't say as I have. Fact is, I've taken up working for the local king there. This Rollaugr, he's called. Got more than his fair share of troubles, he does."

Huh. Well, that was ... not what she'd expected. "If you're working for the king, why are you here?"

"Holmgard is looking to fall soon, I reckon. King's getting fair desperate, and I told him I'd help as best I could. But he's heard of Eightarms here, and he wants him. Was planning to send a man across the Gandvik to come and look for you. So I told him I knew the both of you and I'd come myself."

Starkad passed the horn on and rubbed the back of his hand on his mouth. "What's he want with me?"

"Reckon the same as any king wants with a mercenary. Best you let him do the telling of it, though. I'm only here 'cause I reckoned you'd be more like to help if it was me asking than some stranger."

Probably true. And either way, if they helped Höfund with this, maybe she'd get the chance to recruit him to help deal with the Arrow's Point. "Seems like we have to go," she said.

Starkad glanced at her. "I didn't expect you to agree so readily."

She shrugged. "We owe him." Which was true. "And I know you." Even more true. "You'd have gone regardless."

And there Höfund was, grinning again.

## 13

The growing ache in her shoulders began to overwhelm the throbbing pain in her head and back. Hervor cracked open one eye. The other seemed crusted shut with blood and wouldn't respond. Manacles bound her wrists and strung her up from the ceiling. She was in a cell of some sort, lit—barely lit—by candles on a shelf along the wall.

Afrid was there too, still unconscious from the look of her, and strung up just like Hervor.

A closed metal door shut them in here.

"I can smell that you wake." The words came from shadows beside the door. A man strode forward, the very faint glimmer of candlelight reflecting off his eyes. He wore a robe, elaborate as Tanna's had been, but cut in a different style. Indeed, this one's facial features were different, his skin darker, more like Afzal's had been, though it seemed unlikely he was a Serklander if the two empires were at war.

Hervor grunted in discomfort. "Are you one of them?"

"Them?" The shadowy figure chuckled.

Of course he was one of them. With her head all fuzzy, she was asking pointless questions. "You work for Tanna?"

Now the vampire's expression turned into a sneer. "You are here to answer questions, not to ask them. Tell me what you are doing in Miklagard."

"Ugh. Selling wolf pelts." She looked up at her chains. "Clearly they're not in fashion here, though."

"Arete."

"Huh?" Hervor asked.

A faint disturbance in the air as something passed close behind her, then a female form took shape.

"The next words I hear from her shall be the truth," the vampire said.

"Of course," the female said.

Come to think of it, they were speaking Northern. So that whole exchange was for her benefit. Meaning ...

The lord—another Patriarch, probably—threw open the door and left, not bothering to shut it behind him. They didn't feel the need to lock their victims inside. Because they knew a human woman would never overpower a vampire?

"So," Hervor said. "In my land, the best way to get to know new friends is over drinks."

Arete—assuming that was her name—smiled, revealing fangs. "As you wish." She leaned in close to Hervor's face. Brushed her cheek along Hervor's arm. They'd removed her mail, she suddenly realized. Made sense they'd have taken it with her runeblade.

The female vampire snatched Hervor's sleeve. A single jerk of her hand tore the seams and the sleeve came away. Arete pulled it up, exposing Hervor's left biceps. Without further warning, the vampire bit down on Hervor's arm.

Her fangs punched through flesh with ease, scraped the bone, even.

Hervor shrieked at the burning, piercing agony of it. For an instant. Then it felt like the creature was sucking all the warmth right out of her. Ice welled in Hervor's chest. So cold her scream died in her throat. It felt like her very life was fading away, consumed and devoured with each passing heartbeat. And even her heart began to slow.

"Hel's fucking arse cheeks!" Afrid shouted, the sound muffled, far away.

Arete jerked away, blood dribbling from her lips and down her chin. She licked at it with a bright red tongue, smiled, fluttering her eyes like she was on the verge of a climax.

Hervor convulsed, unable to still shivers that seized her. So cold …

"So …" Arete ran her thumb over her chin, mopping up more blood, then sucked on it. "Lord Nikolaos asked you a question."

"What was the fucking question?" Afrid asked.

Arete snickered and drifted over to the other shield-maiden. "Why? Do you have the answer? You weren't the one with the runeblade …" She leaned in close and sniffed Afrid's neck. "Still. I'm deeply interested to know more about you."

"Huh. Well, unless you have a cock the size of a bear's, I'm probably not interested in you being so close."

Arete chuckled, shaking her head. "How deliciously vulgar you North Realmers are. A cock? No. But I have a skillful tongue. There's actually quite excellent blood flow in your nethers. A little nip where your thigh meets the groin and we could know each other so very well. People have been known to beg for it, after a while …"

Hervor finally managed to blink her other eye open,

though everything was hazy from her blood loss. "Leave her alone."

Arete trailed a long nail over Afrid's cheek, drawing a line of blood as she did so. Afrid grimaced but didn't cry out.

That was enough. "Listen, you sick, dead bitch—" Hervor began.

In a heartbeat Arete was there, holding Hervor's chin so tight it felt like her jaw bones would crack. "I want you to understand something, Northerner. I could pry open your teeth with one hand and rip out your tongue with the other to leave you choking to death on your own blood. Lord Nikolaos would forgive that. He's got lots more of you to interrogate. The local man. The pompous one." She sneered. "The filthy *dog*. The one with a dead eye."

Starkad.

"Oh," Arete said. "Oh, is that one special to you? Hmm." She stalked back over to Afrid. Then she punched her in the gut.

Afrid seized up, clearly trying to double over and unable to do so. Breath exploded from her mouth, followed by wheezing. Gurgling. Coughing out blood in great heaving splatters.

"And does *this* one matter to you, too?" Arete shrugged. "We have all night if that's what it takes. Or I can bring in the man you care for. Maybe break a few bones. Or would it be harder for you to watch if I drain him dry?"

The thought of that set an even colder chill growing in her gut. She couldn't lose Starkad. Not like this.

Arete dug a nail into Afrid's shoulder. The woman squealed, sucking in breaths that obviously pained her.

"Enough," Hervor said. "Enough. What do you want?"

Arete's hand only tightened on Afrid's shoulder. "Why

are you in Miklagard?" Hervor could barely hear the vampire over Afrid's screams of agony.

"We came to steal Tanna's runeblade."

The vampire released Afrid, whose screams rapidly became whimpers. "Runeblade?"

"The sword he carries. It was forged during the time of the Old Kingdoms, by dvergar. We came to reclaim it."

Arete licked the tips of her lips then strode for the door. She flung it open and slammed it behind her, leaving Hervor and Afrid alone in the candlelight.

Afrid was sobbing now, but after losing so much blood, Hervor found it damn hard to focus on aught. She just needed a little rest ...

Maybe she dozed—or fainted—because when the door flew open again, Hervor jolted. How much time had passed? Arete hardly glanced at her. The vampire leapt to the wall and stuck on it. She climbed up the surface like a gods-damned spider, transferred to the ceiling, and crawled along that too.

What the fuck?

The vampire grabbed Hervor's chains off the metal hook they dangled from, hefted her up, then let her drop to the floor. Hervor collapsed, too weak to even consider trying to escape. The sudden removal of the pain in her arms only served to remind her how much they ached.

Arete next dropped Afrid, who crumpled into a heap. Blood was still oozing from the wound on the woman's shoulder.

Before Hervor could even say aught to the other shield-maiden, the vampire dropped off the ceiling and landed between them. She grabbed each of them by an arm, yanked them to their feet, and began dragging them along with her.

Hervor struggled to walk, if only to avoid the indignity of being hauled like a carcass. Afrid seemed to be faring little better.

The vampire guided the pair of them along a dimly lit corridor for several dozen feet before shoving them through an open door. They both stumbled, pitched to the floor, and landed on hands and knees.

Groaning, Hervor lifted her head. The room within was cleaner than anywhere else down in these sewers, if still unadorned stone. Nikolaos sat in an ornate chair, one leg crossed over the other, fingers drumming on the armrests.

"Hervor," Starkad said, coming to her side and helping her up.

Höfund moved to help Afrid, but she shoved him away, glaring at Nikolaos.

Hervor leaned on Starkad, too fucking tired to care overmuch on pride anymore.

The others were there, too, standing against the side wall. Vebiorg's hands were behind her back. Manacled? So the vampires respected the varulf's strength enough to keep her bound, while fearing naught from the humans.

"So," Nikolaos said. "I am given to understand you came to Miklagard because of a grievance against my fellow Patriarch."

Starkad grunted, maybe surprised.

Maybe Hervor shouldn't have said aught, but it seemed better to be out with it than get tortured more and then reveal the truth anyway. Or to have to watch Arete torture Starkad.

Win almost snarled at the Patriarch. "Tanna has dared

strike against lands under the protection of the Aesir. He has badly overreached himself."

Nikolaos snickered. "It seems to me you are the ones who overreached at the moment."

Win spat. How princely of him. "Even if we fail, others will come. The Aesir will not let your corruption spread across Midgard."

Now Nikolaos broke into a full chuckle, shaking his head. "Blood of Kvasir, human! Who do you think you are? Your precious, dear Ás king himself was here not a moon back. He fled, bloody and weak, no doubt hiding on his far-flung islands."

"Blasphemous lies!" Win shouted.

Odin had come here? Had fought these creatures? Had … lost?

Even Starkad seemed shaken, had drawn in a sharp breath at Nikolaos's comments. No, the vampire lord didn't seem to be lying. But Hervor found it hard to fathom or credence that a god could have come here and failed. Would that not make the Patriarchs themselves … gods?

Nikolaos leaned back, clearly not interested in disputing his claims with Win. His smirk said it all.

Arete, meanwhile, stalked in front of the crew, looking each up and down with a sneer. "They cannot do it. Most of them are *human*." The sheer contempt with which she said the last word left Hervor reeling. How far removed this creature must have been from her own humanity.

Or … well, Hervor was assuming that like draugar, vampires had once been human. Perhaps they were aught else entirely. Hardly mattered, really.

"Cannot do what?" Baruch asked.

Nikolaos's smug grin only deepened. "If outsiders came here and slew Tanna, it might open opportunities for those

Patriarchs who remained. Voids in the structure of society. No such void can long exist, and thus, those who are most prepared would be best able to take advantage."

Starkad grunted. "You mean you want us to kill Tanna so you can move in on his territory."

"A vast oversimplification of political structures more ancient and more complicated than you might begin to fathom, mortal."

Maybe it was Hervor's imagination, but it seemed Arete cast an almost concealed glance between Starkad and Nikolaos. Something hidden, even from her lord?

"Suppose we could do it," Starkad said. "What would you offer us?"

"Your lives and freedom."

Hervor groaned. "Just let us leave. Coming here was a mistake."

Arete snorted at that. "I can see what he sees in you, shieldmaiden. You have utterly mastered the blisteringly obvious."

Hervor glared at the female vampire but had little energy to do aught more.

"Last time we faced Tanna, things went amiss," Starkad said. Kind of understating it, wasn't he? "What can you offer us to ensure our success?"

"A hidden route into his palace."

"His tower?"

Nikolaos waved that away. "You think he owns but one dwelling in the whole of the city? No. You are more like to catch him unawares if you strike in a different location. Even now, he has his agents hunting you. Had they found you before mine stumbled upon you, you would be having this conversation with him. Tanna might be less amenable to your mission than myself. Considerably so."

No. No. No. "This is mist-madness," she whispered to Starkad. "We've lost enough. Let us flee this place."

Nikolaos quirked an eyebrow as if he'd heard that. "What will it be, then?"

Starkad blew out a long breath. "We agree to your terms."

The vampire lord uncrossed his legs and leaned forward. "I will have an oath on your blood that you will not leave this city until the deed is done."

"So be it," Starkad said.

Arete drew close to him then snatched his wrist. He grimaced as she bit down.

Starkad held up his arm, allowing blood to dribble down it to the floor. "I give you my oath on my own blood, I will not leave Miklagard until I have slain Lord Tanna."

Nikolaos chuckled. "Wonderful. Let us begin."

## 14

Two Moons Ago

No one could much deny hard times had fallen on Holmgard. Worse even than when last Hervor had come through, some two years back. The population seemed shrunken, less than before. Maybe too many had died, maybe they'd begun to abandon this colony, come back to Sviarland.

Word of Gylfi's death would've reached them by now, maybe made things worse. The sorcerer king had ordered this colony founded. After his son-in-law died, Rollaugr's father had come to power and the kingdom had flourished —more or less. But now, so many houses stood empty. Boats left in disrepair. Some buildings had logs missing from them, like people had just claimed them for firewood.

Despite it all, Rollaugr received them warmly, offering up a table of fresh perch and mead—if the latter seemed a bit watery to Hervor's taste. The king himself sat across the table from them, barely touching his own food so intent was he on watching Starkad.

Höfund tore into his plate with his usual relish, slobbering like a wolf with a fresh kill. She'd mostly gotten used to it, anyway. Still, she'd avoided letting him catch her alone on the voyage here. It wasn't hard—longships didn't offer overmuch in the way of privacy. Even Höfund seemed wise enough not to mention his proposal for her hand in front of the crew.

Hervor took another swig of the disappointing mead before passing it to a green-eyed shieldmaiden beside her.

A slave whispered something in the king's ear and he nodded, offered some answer Hervor couldn't catch. Rollaugr looked apt to burst from his request, but tradition dictated he offer guests food before business, and he was clearly a man of tradition.

"Is it true you bear a runeblade, shieldmaiden?" he asked.

Damn. Did he know it for the very blade once held by this same kingdom? Hervor struggled to keep her face neutral. "I do."

"I might very much like to see it. Perhaps when you have eaten."

She stared at her fish.

Starkad grunted and shoved his plate away. "I for one have had my fill. Tell me, king, why did you send Höfund for us?"

Before Rollaugr could answer, another man strode into the hall. A young man, with travel-worn clothes and armor bearing the scuffs of battle. The king rose and embraced the young man, who returned the gesture. It was a moment before either of them looked back to Starkad. When Rollaugr did, he outstretched a hand toward the other man. "My son, Win, just returned from the front lines."

"Front lines?" Hervor asked. "Are you at war?" Numerous

petty jotunn kings had carved up most of Bjarmaland between them, but, so far as she knew, none had yet invaded Holmgard. If they had, she didn't see how the kingdom would yet be standing at all.

"At war, yes," Win said. "Soldiers of Miklagard strike out further and further with each passing summer. We had to hold our outposts in the south until we were certain they'd retired for the winter. When the snows melt ..." Win looked to his father. "We cannot hold out another season."

Miklagard? The great South Realmer empire was the stuff of legend as far as Hervor knew.

"They push out from Kaunos?" Starkad asked.

"Yes, but that's only a staging ground for these godless barbarians. The real threat comes from the city of Miklagard itself. So removed they think themselves untouchable."

Rollaugr cleared his throat. "We rather hope you can prove them wrong."

Starkad grunted. "You mean to mount an attack on the city of Miklagard itself? That bespeaks mist-madness, king, if you'll forgive my bluntness. Even could we muster all the warriors of Sviarland, I doubt we could take and hold that city."

Win sat at the table beside his father. "We need neither sack nor hold Miklagard. With Odin's blessing, we need merely strike a blow against them such that they realize we are not helpless prey. Let them set their ambitions elsewhere and leave us in peace."

Hervor frowned. "What possible blow do you imagine will dissuade them?"

Win glanced her way and quirked a smile, though no hint of mirth reached his eyes. "We know their empire is governed by leaders they call Patriarchs. One of these, Lord

Tanna, is responsible for Kaunos and the incursions made through there."

"You aim to murder him," Starkad said, voice so flat Hervor couldn't guess whether he approved or not.

"I aim to bring the wrath of the Aesir down them," Win said. "Reports claim Tanna holds a sword of the North Realms. One of dire strength, engraved with strange markings the Miklagardians do not understand."

Starkad leaned forward. "A runeblade?"

Odin's stones. If there was any chance of not doing this, it was gone now. Hervor rubbed her temples. Starkad would never pass up the chance to claim his own runeblade.

"It stands to reason," Rollaugr said. "We want you to infiltrate Miklagard and kill Tanna. Then we hope his replacement is more timid."

Starkad rubbed his palms together and glanced at Hervor. She could shake her head. Could try to talk him out of this—it was clearly mist-madness. The Holmgarders weren't trying to hire him to fight a battle or hold off any enemy. They were sending him well beyond known lands into Odin alone knew what. But Starkad would never back down. Never could, maybe. So what point in her arguing with him over it?

Instead, Hervor put her hands on the table. "We'd need a hefty payment for this. Three times Starkad's weight in gold. Plus we keep the runeblade."

Win blanched, looked to his father.

The king closed his eyes, groaned. "So be it."

Starkad clapped Hervor on the shoulder. "Good, then. I'll need to put together my own crew."

"You can choose who you like," Win said. "But I'm going. And Tveggi goes where I go." Win inclined his head to an aging warrior lingering by the entrance. A thegn? A bodyguard?

Starkad frowned. "This is hardly going to be safe, prince. Perhaps you had best remain here where—"

"I am no craven. With Odin's blessing, we will find glory. And if I fall, valkyries will carry me to Valhalla."

Sounded a small comfort to Hervor, but Win seemed so sincere she had to bite her tongue.

"Well," Höfund said, "reckon I'm going too. Can't rightly let aught happen to the pair of you nor the prince neither."

"I'll go too," the shieldmaiden beside Hervor said.

Hervor had almost forgotten her in the rush of events. "Who are you?"

"Vebiorg."

Hervor looked to Starkad, who frowned. "Hervor and I will meet with any willing to go in the morn. We need keep our numbers small if we hope to pass ourselves off as mere travelers. Just enough warriors that we can handle opposition when we face it."

Rollaugr cleared his throat. "It's decided then." He turned to a slave. "Arrange chambers for our guests." Now he looked back to her. "I am still interested to look upon the runeblade."

Hervor grimaced. There really was naught to do save tell the truth. "These blades have a will of their own. It is unwise to draw them unless you intend to use them."

Rollaugr pursed his lips. Did he recognize her description of Tyrfing's curse? Did he know of that specific runeblade? He shrugged then, and shook his head. "Pity. Well then, perhaps some more mead before we retire?"

Hervor could go for that indeed.

# PART II

Eleventh Moon
Year 31, Age of the Aesir

## 15

The tunnels beneath the city seemed to stretch on endlessly. Parts of them criss-crossed the sewers, but other regions—such as those corridors Arete now led Starkad and his crew through—remained mostly dry, if still grimy.

Nikolaos had vanished into the darkness, but the female vampire had stuck by Starkad's side, guiding them to Nikolaos's palace. The sun would be up any moment, she had explained, and the vampires preferred not to go out in daylight, much like draugar.

He had a crude bandage wrapped around his wrist where she'd bit him, holding a torch with his other hand.

"You fear the light?" he asked.

"I ... fear naught ... mortal."

"You hesitate."

"And you," she whispered, her voice so low the others behind probably couldn't catch it—save Vebiorg. "You are not quite mortal, are you?"

He tried to stifle his surprise at her words, but there was no denying his pulse quickened at hearing them. Odin had extended his life. When Arete had bitten him—back when she was interrogating him—she'd reacted strangely, as if shocked by the taste. Maybe whatever Odin had done had changed him more than Starkad realized. He was fortified. If not so much as he would've been with an apple of Yggdrasil, still heartier than an ordinary man.

"I've had a long, complex life," he finally answered.

"Oh? Most of my kind can say the same." She led him around another bend, beyond which lay stone steps rising up. She climbed them with uncanny grace, seeming almost to glide to the top, where she inserted a key into a trapdoor in the ceiling. After turning it, she threw the hatch open, and continued up.

Starkad followed her up into a cellar that, compared to the tunnels below, was shockingly clean and free of dust and grime. As he stood, he noticed a circle painted around the trapdoor in what looked like semi-fresh blood. Around its perimeter, runes ran. Sorcery? He grimaced.

"A ward against intruders," Arete answered his unspoken question.

The others joined him up in the cellar, each looking around. Höfund examined the circle with obvious distaste, and Hervor blanched when she noticed it.

Arete led them out of the cellar and into a corridor, this one flanked by a half dozen guards.

So. The vampires used the tunnels to get around in daylight. Knowing this, Nikolaos used special protections to ward the potential weak point in his palace. Just what did those wards do?

Beyond the corridor, they went up yet more steps, into corridors painted white and decorated with golden trim. Tapestries and paintings lined the walls, even before the passage opened up into a wide hall with a high ceiling. An upper level looked down on this hall, supported by columns engraved to look like nude men and women in the throes of various acts of passion.

The sheer decadence of the palace, from the marble columns to the lush tapestries to the gold trim on the rails—all of it—fair reeked of hubris. As if Nikolaos needed to flaunt his god-like wealth despite the squalor and filth so much of the city lived in. Pompous, consciously so, in fact.

And there were no windows.

"You will wish to rest from your travels and ... ordeals," Arete said. "We will not strike in daylight, in any event."

"Wouldn't Tanna be weaker then?"

"Yes. But he will also be in hiding and not even we know where to seek him out. No, unfortunately, you must draw out the Patriarch before you can engage him. In the meantime, I'll show you each to your chambers."

THE OTHERS SETTLED IN, Arete led Starkad to a room on the upper levels. "You're their leader."

"Yes."

"So was it your idea to come here, so far from your own lands?"

He shrugged. He'd been farther than this from the North Realms. Much farther, if he counted the sojourn Ogn had taken his soul on through the Otherworlds. "I was hired for it."

"Oh. A mercenary." She opened the door to a room decorated with half again more luxury than he needed. A plush bed, a dresser the color of olives. A wash basin of solid bronze. A man-sized cupboard for who knew what.

"Mercenary. Wanderer. Whatever you want to call me."

Arete shut the door with the both of them inside.

Starkad turned to her. She was running her tongue over her teeth, lingering it over those fangs. Hard to deny it sent his pulse quickening, which no doubt was her intent.

"What do you want?"

She edged closer. Close enough he could feel just a hint of warmth to her. Strange, draugar were cold as the grave. Why wasn't she? "I can feel your heartbeat. Thrumming ... throbbing ..." She craned her neck on the last word, a hairsbreadth from his cheek. Meaning he couldn't even see her because of his dead eye.

The thought of Hervor in the next room sent him falling back several steps. "Didn't you suggest I rest?"

"By all means ... use the bed." She flicked her tongue out over her lower lip.

He frowned. Doubly so at the mental image of taking her that leapt unbidden to his mind. "I'm bound to Hervor."

Arete snickered. "If that's the life you want. Bound to a single *human* woman when we both know something more than that lies deep in your blood. Something dark and succulent and powerful, waiting to come out. Do you truly wish to spend the rest of your days wandering Midgard?"

"I ... That's my curse." Why was he even telling her this?

"Is that what you tell yourself? A half-truth to hide from the bitter reality that, as yet, you have found naught in this world capable of satisfying you." She traced a finger down her jawline, and over one breast. Pursed her lips. "Nor will you, among the world of ordinary men. Ordinary ... women. How would someone blessed with such gifts as I taste in you be sated with the cold blandness found out there?"

He was already shaking his head. No. It wasn't true. He wandered because he was cursed to do so. He *couldn't* have contentment. Couldn't have a place in the world to himself.

That was the price of his long life and extraordinary constitution. And that was all there was to it.

What Arete suggested ... that somewhere ... that *here* might offer him something he'd been missing ... No. He refused to accept that. He wandered because that was his urd, decided the moment he'd killed Vikar, if not before.

Made certain when he'd failed Ogn.

"You should go," he said.

Arete frowned, ever so slightly. "Consider this. I have walked over much of this world. When I was young, I remember refugees fleeing the collapse of what you call the Old Kingdoms. They came through our lands, burning and pillaging, taking who and what they desired. They burned my home and killed my family, and I wandered, too. Whoring myself to survive. Until I came here. On the streets I might've died, had not Nikolaos found me. And brought me a new life." She shook her head. "I was not so very different from you, long centuries ago."

"You're saying you're eight *hundred* winters old?"

She snickered, gliding to the door. "Maybe I'm twenty-five winters. Maybe I'll be twenty-five winters old from now until the end of time." She had a hand on the handle. "The point is, my wanderings ended here. Yours could as well, should you so desire it."

Without another word, she slipped out of the room and left him alone.

## 16

*H*ervor was leaning on the rail, looking down on the grand hall below, when that vampire bitch slipped out of Starkad's room. Arete caught her looking and smiled smugly.

Odin's treacherous stones, no. No, that wasn't going to happen. Hervor pushed off the rail and stormed over to the bitch. "What in Hel's icy trench are you about now?"

Arete smiled, the expression not reaching her cold eyes. "You speak to me as if you think I am like you. Somehow, you dare to forget that, on a whim, I could put my little finger through your windpipe before you knew I was moving."

Hervor couldn't help but grimace at that mental image. Over her shoulder, Tyrfing begged her to draw it. To let the pale flames engulf this undead abomination. From what she'd seen on Thule, one cut didn't poison a draug like it did a man. But the blade managed to kill draugar as if they were men. So if she hacked out Arete's bowels, would the vampire bleed out?

"Do not test me," the vampire warned. Reading her face?

Hervor forced a confident smirk to her face. "I was going to say the same."

Starkad had made a blood oath to Nikolaos. Maybe he'd had no choice. Either way, she couldn't see how they could possibly trust these monstrous things. A vampire had slaughtered Fjolvor and Tveggi like they were pigs. These creatures fed off people. They were every bit as loathsome as the worst vaettir.

That they could pass for human almost made them more abhorrent. Like, once she knew of their nature, she couldn't help but notice a subtle wrongness about Arete. Though Hervor could not point to any one thing, just looking at the creature filled her with unease.

"Hmm. You think you have claim on him. You think you, a mere mortal woman, can hold on to a man whose blood is suffused with dark power. But you fool yourself and—for now—you fool him. But these delusions cannot last nor end well. You build your imagined future on spider strands of lies that must inevitably snap beneath their own weight."

Hervor glared at her. "I *do* have claim on him. Our oaths bind us together."

"Mortal oaths are but fragile things. Given time, they all break."

"Not ours." She could barely stop her twitching fingers from reaching for Tyrfing. Oh, how she wanted to end this bitch.

"We shall see." Arete brushed past Hervor then.

As the vampire passed, Hervor reached up for the runeblade. One chance. Draw and strike in a single swift movement. She might just be fast enough ...

And then Arete was too far away, sauntering along the balcony without bothering to cast another glance behind her. As if Hervor was beneath further notice.

Hervor ground her teeth.

Below, on the lower level, footfalls echoed off the marble floor. Hervor returned to the balcony to see Höfund down there, gaping at the columns.

Maybe Hervor ought to check in on Starkad. Find out what Arete had really said to him. But ... part of her feared to even hear it. Everything with him was so hard these days.

That they loved each other ought to have been enough.

Maybe ... Maybe when this was done, they could finally settle down. Maybe he could get a handle on his curse, take control. She had to believe that. For now, perhaps giving him time was the best thing. Or the easiest, at least.

So she tromped down a winding staircase to the lower floor.

Höfund looked up at her approach. "Reminds me a bit of jotunn kingdoms."

The decor didn't look aught like Godmund's palace to her. "How so?"

Höfund folded his arms. "Bit overmuch, all this. Wealth gathered from all around the domain. Some of it tribute, some of it stolen, taken by force and what have you." He wandered over to a tapestry depicting a battle in which both sides sat mounted on numerous horses. "Different in the specifics, 'course. I mean to say, just similar in being too ... too ..."

"Pompous?"

"Reckon so, assuming that word means what I reckon it means."

Hervor nodded. "Why serve Rollaugr, Höfund? You could've gone anywhere, done aught you wished in Midgard? Why take up with a doomed king in a faltering kingdom?"

"Huh. Can't say as I looked at it much from that direction. More like I saw a half-decent man—decent as the world lets a man be, leastwise—and saw him hard-pressed by my own kin. And I reckoned maybe I could do somewhat about that and make my fortune all at one go."

Make his fortune. She shook her head and sighed. She'd spent a good many years trying to do the same. Leading raids, playing pirate. Never amounted to overmuch, really. Sure, she'd taken her share of plunder, but it never lasted long. There was always more on the horizon. At least until Thule ...

Or until after that. Until she and Starkad had gotten all twined up in each other. And by then, she was so sick of the life ... of seeing everyone around her die awful deaths. Almost hard to imagine the kind of woman she'd been before. A murderous bitch who killed for the sport of it, who took whatever she wanted. Who hardly noticed when her crew raped or slaughtered along the way.

But even if she wanted to leave it behind, even if this job somehow did give her the wealth to buy back her grandfather's fortunes, still something remained to keep her from peace. Something that had followed her into this very gods-damned city.

Hervor glanced around the hall to make sure no one was about. Not behind the columns, not on the balcony. A couple of slaves passed by overhead, not dawdling in the least nor even looking in her direction. "There's something I need your help with."

The big man blew out a heaving breath. "Reckon I'd help with just about aught. Ain't got that many friends and I aim to keep those I have."

Well, she couldn't help but smile at that. Maybe she should be honest with him, first. Tell him she'd never marry him. But breaking all his hopes was like to send him into melancholy. Besides interfering with her request, that might well get the half-jotunn killed given what Starkad had agreed to. Tonight, they'd be fighting a godsdamned vampire lord, after all.

No, she couldn't tell him that. Not now, not here. "I, uh ... I killed a man."

Höfund shrugged. "Ain't we all?"

"This one deserved it." She looked around again. "He did, but still I wish I hadn't done it. Because he was known to ... some of the others. They wouldn't take it well and I don't want them to know it."

Höfund sniffed. "I ain't a fool, me. You can come out and say it's Eightarms you're fretting over."

"Right. The thing is ... this man, he ... He came back."

Now Höfund screwed up his face in an expression that might've set his enemies shitting their trousers. "You didn't burn the corpse? A boy barely off his mother's teat knows you don't leave a body in the mist."

She flinched. Yes, she should've known. "I was a little preoccupied with an army of draugar trying to kill me and my crew."

"Sure. And now that army's got one more in their number, that it?"

"That's the gist. He's been harrying my steps ever since. Hurting those I care about. I tried to fight him but ..."

The half-jotunn shook his head. "Right then. Reckon I've done my share of damn fool deeds now and again, so I can't hardly hold that against you. So you're wanting my help sending the draug back to the grave, permanent this time. And wanting it without anyone else finding out the lout even exists."

"Pretty much."

Höfund shrugged. "Well, like I said. I'd help with just

about aught you needed, Hervor. When we make it back to the North Realms, once this is done, I'll help you hunt the draug."

"Uh … he's here."

"Huh. Makes things a bit more troublesome, don't it?"

Hervor nodded.

He let a meaty hand fall on her shoulder. "I see any draugar, I'll chop 'em clean in half. Work for you?"

She couldn't help but smile. "You're a good friend."

"Huh. Reckon so."

## 17

Two Moons Ago

*A* throng of warriors, men and women both, had gathered in Rollaugr's hall. The king himself was not here, though, and Win sat on his throne instead, seeming fair lost in thought. Tveggi stood beside him, glowering at the crowd as if any one of them might suddenly lunge at the prince.

They'd granted Hervor a chair before the throne. One for Starkad too, but he instead paced about the hall, inciting the warriors about the glory of the mission and the chance for plunder. Like as not, a good many of those who went might die. Maybe they'd all die. Then there wouldn't be the least bit of plunder, nor anyone to tell the truth of their stories.

A morbid thought, true, but the more Hervor heard of Win's tales of Miklagard, the more she misliked the whole damn plan. Starkad intended to sail into port posing as merchants and their guards. The Miklagardian walls were said to be massive, so the port was the only approach, really.

The locals would search the ship, of course. Meaning their crew had to bring cargo actually worth selling. Unfortunately, no one here seemed to know much of any real details about the city or its people. They'd be going in half-blind, nigh as she could tell. Didn't bode well. None of this did.

Still, she'd promised to help Höfund, and she wouldn't break that promise. And if they managed to pull through, maybe she could get a promise out of him, too. Maybe he'd judge her when she told him about Orvar. Maybe he wouldn't want to wed her anymore—hardly a loss there. But if he could help her put an end to the draug without Starkad finding out, it'd be worth it.

"All Starkad Eightarms has said is true," Win said, rising. "Ahead of us we may find glory fit to sate even an Ás. Though too, you must be prepared to gaze into the very gates of Hel before you see Valhalla." He strode down beside Starkad. "Many of you have fought the Miklagardians. What lies ahead of us will not be like what you faced before. And still I ask you to stride forward, ready to meet the Aesir if that is your urd."

Hervor frowned. She'd almost met an Ás at Gylfi's funeral. And Starkad didn't seem overfond of the man. The more she saw of the world, the less sense it all made. Maybe all that mattered was carving out a piece for yourself. She'd do so, and damn the cost.

Vebiorg shoved her way through the crowd almost as soon as Win finished speaking. "You know you need me."

Win stiffened. Didn't like the shieldmaiden? Maybe he'd fucked her once or something. Either way, the woman seemed bold enough and had the build of someone used to swinging that axe hanging from her belt.

Hervor rose from her seat and joined the others. "What makes you better than the rest?"

Vebiorg cast a sneering glance back at the gathered throng of warriors. Those closest to her actually backed away a few steps. "I'm stronger, tougher, and faster than any man here."

Huh. Bold claim. But then, Hervor liked bold. "Does she speak true?"

Win glanced at Hervor. "Vebiorg is ... a varulf."

Oh, Odin's stones. Varulfur in Skane had torn through Hervor's crew there like they were sheep. She still had gods-damned nightmares about that night from time to time. It was all she could do to keep her face even.

Starkad managed even less. "We don't need varulfur."

"She does speak true," Win said. Hervor had almost forgotten her original question.

While she didn't fancy having a varulf around, someone that strong, that fast ... on their side. It could prove a boon. "How does a varulf come into the service of the king of Holmgard?"

"Long story," Vebiorg said. "Maybe I'll tell you one day. Your best odds of success are with me, and you all know it. I can hunt. I can track. And I can kill Miklagardians better than anyone else."

Starkad took a step toward her. "Not better than *anyone*."

"She's in," Hervor said before Starkad could dismiss her. Varulfur might be the stuff skalds threw in tales to scare people, true, but their mission seemed dire enough without turning away those with superhuman abilities.

A light rumble ran through the gathered throng, and someone else came shoving her way forward. A girl, maybe seventeen winters on her, though she had a scar across her cheek and her mail looked well-worn. "You can't take her and not me!"

Now Starkad actually rolled his eyes.

"Leave the children at home," another man said. He had dark hair and deeper skin, almost as deep as Afzal had. "If you're going up against Miklagard, you need someone familiar with it. I grew up on those city streets."

A Miklagardian?

"If that's so," Starkad said, "how are we to trust you?"

The man smirked. "I never got aught from those streets save beatings and runny shits. Eventually I was shipped off to Kaunos and got caught in a raid. King Rollaugr took me—maybe the best thing that ever happened to me."

A woman had grabbed his arm and was trying to pull him back into the crowd. The Miklagardian pulled her forward instead. "I'm sure my wife will want to come too."

The woman, another shieldmaiden maybe, grimaced before offering a wan smile.

A well-muscled man stepped forward. "Bunch of former slaves are hardly enough when things turn to troll shit. You need someone who can crack some skulls."

Hervor had to admit, the man looked like someone who could do just that, and probably enjoyed himself in the process.

"Fine," Starkad said to him. "You as well. That should be enough."

"Wait," the young girl objected. "You haven't even seen what I can do."

The big man scoffed.

Then the girl kicked him in his stones. An instant later her fist cracked him on the ear. Hervor wouldn't have thought a little thing like her could fell an oaf like that. But he just toppled over, one hand to his groin, the other to his no-doubt-ringing ear.

"Yeah, you're in," Hervor said.

Starkad turned on her, mouth open. Maybe he was going to object to her choosing the girl over the oaf. She silently dared him to say as much. But Starkad just shrugged.

"What's your name?" Hervor asked.

"Afrid. Afrid the … uh … Well, I haven't fastened a name yet, but don't think I won't!"

Hervor quirked a smile. Had she herself been like that a few winters back? "Afrid Stonekicker." A few chuckles from the crowd. "Welcome to the crew."

MAYBE NONE of this was quite what Hervor had imagined when she'd agreed to come with Höfund. Maybe, but here they were, sitting in Rollaugr's hall, while Höfund and Baruch—the Miklagardian—gathered supplies to leave in the morn.

Four dogsleds, Starkad had said, two people to a sled. They'd have to go as far as they could toward Kaunos and get a ship there to carry them across the Black Sea. A long voyage, and not one she expected to go smoothly.

"This is it, right?" she said.

Starkad was fiddling with a brazier, but he looked up at her. "Huh?"

"I mean, we do this job, get rich. Use the gold to rebuild Grandfather's lands, or maybe buy a title from another king. Something. But no more of this afterward."

Starkad groaned. "You know … that's not how it works with me. I cannot make any such promise, Hervor. No matter my intent, the wanderlust always comes back. Nor can I long seem to hold wealth."

"You don't have to. I will."

"You know who I am. I never made the least secret of it."

"Well, you can still *try* to change. Grandfather has been asking me to stop the wanderings, to—"

Starkad stood up abruptly, turned his back on her and stormed from the hall.

Odin's godsdamned stones. What would it take?

"Waiting for him to wed you?" Fjolvor asked.

Hervor started. She hadn't even realized Baruch's wife was in here. "It's more complicated than that with us."

Fjolvor shrugged. "I married a freed Miklagardian slave. I get complicated."

"You don't even really want to go, do you?"

The other woman offered a fake smile. "Sometimes people do things they don't want to in order to help the ones they love."

Didn't Hervor know it.

## 18

*M*uch like draugar, vampires lost many of their superhuman abilities in sunlight. Fortunately for Orvar, they countered this weakness by constructing a network of tunnels under Miklagard. Mostly, only vampire cast-offs lived down in the so-called undercity. Those fallen out of favor with the Patriarchs, perhaps scurrying to try any tactic to redeem themselves.

Then, though, there remained some few human enclaves who operated with the sufferance of their vampire overlords by paying tribute in gold and perhaps, in blood. As with this faltering hovel of shanties clustered around a wide chamber beneath the markets. These people were thieves and beggars so wretched they could not even lurk in the alleys above ground.

Perhaps they didn't know what lurked down here. Perhaps they thought anywhere out of the open was better than being on the streets at night. A man with a pockmarked face wormed his way against the back wall, as if he might escape from the confines Orvar had trapped him in.

*Vengeance. Vengeance. Vengeance.*

"I will ask you one more time," Orvar said, leaning close enough for the man to smell the rot coming off him, even over the stench of these tunnels. "Where do I find the foreigners?"

"Don't know shit, I told you."

"Ugh." Orvar seized him by the throat with one hand, hefted him off the ground, and slammed him into the wall.

The ugly man hung motionless for a moment, dazed, no doubt. Then began to wriggle in Orvar's grasp as if he might be able to break it. In truth, the withered and underfed beggar couldn't have gotten free even had Orvar been out in cursed daylight with merely the human strength of his own muscles. Here, in the darkness, the man might as well have been trying to push over a mammoth with his bare hands.

Orvar tightened his grasp, ever so slightly. Enough to bruise the man's throat without actually crushing his windpipe. Beggars and other undesirables knew a lot. That hardly mattered if they couldn't speak.

When he judged the man sufficiently cowed, he released him. The beggar slumped to the ground in a heap, gasping, choking, maybe even sobbing. Hard to be sure what the disgusting mix of guttural noises amounted to. Orvar had no sympathy for the fool's pain. The living could not imagine the eternal agony of the damned. An endless torture abated in only the slightest by visiting suffering on those around them.

*Vengeance. Vengeance. Vengeance.*

"Tell me where to find the foreigners. North Realmers who came on a ship two days back, out of Kaunos. You either know where they are, know who does, or are useless to me. It would be unfortunate for us both if the third option is all we are left with."

The man gasped again. "Verniamin ..."

"What?"

"Verniamin. He sells information from the bath house on Merchant's Street."

Orvar barred his teeth. "If I have to come back here, I will eat your foot and leave you to hobble through this filth. Assuming you survive."

The pock-marked man nodded hesitantly. "Verniamin."

THE TUNNELS CONNECTED to the bath house, leading up into a basement where furnaces heated the waters. The workers down here—slaves, probably—studiously ignored his passage, trained, no doubt, to not meet the gaze of anyone coming up from the tunnels. One would assume that normally included only vampires.

Orvar trod up the stairs and out of the back rooms into the main hall. Curtains blocked off several disparate pools, a few of which were lit by large windows. Other pools, mercifully located on the interior, were lit only by braziers.

A slave bearing a jug passed by, a naked girl of maybe fifteen winters. Orvar snared her elbow.

She uttered a yelp of surprise, quickly stifled, and stared at her feet.

"Where do I find Verniamin?"

At that, the girl started to look up, apparently thought better of it, and pointed at one of the curtains. A pool in the middle of the hall. Excellent. Orvar released the slave and strode through the curtain.

A half dozen naked men and women lounged waist-deep in the pool. One man leaned against the side of the wall, a woman draped over his shoulder and whispering into his ears. He—and several others—looked up at Orvar's entrance and sneered. Maybe at him coming in clad at all, much less in travel-worn clothes, or maybe at him being a foreigner. Hardly mattered, really. Either way, their disdain only made this all the sweeter.

Orvar kicked off his boots, then hopped in the pool without bothering to remove aught else. Mud from his trousers immediately spread around the waters.

"What're you doing?" one of the men demanded.

Orvar looked to him. "Verniamin?"

This one glanced at the man by the side of the pool, with the woman. That was who Orvar had figured, but best to be certain first.

He snatched the closer man's throat and drove him under the waters, holding him there while fixing his gaze on Verniamin. The woman next him shrieked and scrambled out of the pool. Another man and woman blundered gracelessly for the steps.

Orvar ignored them. "I understand you have information."

"You're one of them."

"Distant cousin. I'm going to ask you a question now. You're going to tell me the truth. And then I'm going to leave. If any step in this process does not go as I have laid out, you will find it unpleasant. Do you understand?"

Verniamin nodded. "For fuck's sake, let the man live."

*Vengeance. Vengeance. Vengeance.*

Orvar had almost forgotten about the fool he was drowning. He jerked the man up from under the pool. The bastard was already still in his grasp. With a shrug, Orvar released him. "A group of North Realmers came in two days ago, on a ship from Kaunos. They stirred up trouble and

MATT LARKIN

then they vanished. So, tell me, peddler of information, where did they flee?"

The man's eyes widened a hair. "You mean those imbeciles who broke into Tanna's tower. Word is they were grabbed in the undercity by ... those seeking favor with another of the Patriarchs."

"Which Patriarch?"

"Lord Nikolaos, according to rumor."

Orvar frowned. Did that mean Hervor was dead? What would this Nikolaos do with foreigners who tried to kill another lord? He hadn't handed them over, that much Orvar was fair certain of.

Not granting Verniamin another glance, Orvar left the pool.

"Our society is complex," Tanna said. "Built upon traditions left over from civilizations that turned to dust ages before the coming of the mists. From eras no one remembers, even among my kind. And from them, our customs have blossomed like a garden full of creepers, densely intertwined until we are all choking one another, unable to so much as move."

Orvar glowered, sitting upon one of the Patriarch's lush couches in a hookah den beneath his palace. The couch wasn't comfortable. Naught could ever make Orvar comfortable. His existence was made of pain. "Until an outsider like me comes along to hack away at the excess."

Plumes of smoke from the hookahs drifted around the vampire lord, though he seemed not the least affected by them. "Perhaps, but as I said, we are intertwined. Any such weeding must be done with utmost care, lest you harm growths we hold interest in." The vampire too reclined on a couch, sipping from a goblet Orvar seriously doubted held wine. Crimson droplets dribbled down Tanna's chin. "Nevertheless, an outsider might have his uses. Perhaps, when our mutual enemies are dead, you might find long-term employment in the society of your ... hmm, kindred."

Orvar was fair certain Tanna had intended to say "betters." Vampires might well have had more powers than draugar. They certainly seemed to find eternity less unbearable. But the idea of serving the decadent, self-important lord indefinitely tasted like ash. Indeed, it took studious effort to keep the disdain from his face. "We'll discuss the future once the present has been attended to."

With the hand holding the goblet, Tanna pointed his index finger at Orvar. "You still plan like a mortal. Perhaps in time you will learn to machinate on a grander scale."

Keeping the sneer off his face was getting harder and harder. Orvar didn't give a troll's shit about manipulating societies from the shadows or Miklagardian courtly intrigue. Or this decadent absurdity Tanna lived in. Beside the hookah den lay a massive harem with unclad women and girls from all over the world. Even if Orvar's cock still worked, who the fuck needed forty different women? Did Tanna even know all their names? No, only one thing mattered to Orvar.

*Vengeance. Vengeance. Vengeance.*

Naught else could ever stand next to that all-consuming need. If he was finally sated ... it was hard to even imagine that. "What does Nikolaos want with Hervor?"

Tanna shrugged dismissively. "Perhaps he means to abet her attempt to assassinate me."

"You don't seem overly concerned about that."

"Whatever Nikolaos's play, he wouldn't dare strike against me himself. That leaves only mortals. Barely worth considering. Besides, I already have an agent among them. When they come, I'll be waiting."

## 19

Innumerable books, scrolls, and loose parchments ringed the shelves of the vampire archives. A library unlike aught Starkad had ever seen. Presumably, Arete had brought him here to try to impress him. Since Starkad couldn't read, the effect might have been somewhat less than the vampire had hoped for.

She ran her fingertips over the spines of several books in a row. "Some of these are written in languages so old no one living would even recognize them. Scribed in paper so ancient, we dare not open the volume for fear it would crumble to dust."

"What's the point in a book no one can read?"

"Because these preserve thousands of years of history, tradition. Not only of the vampire race, but of the race of man. Of truths about your own past that you cannot begin to imagine."

Starkad shrugged. "They don't preserve aught. If no one can look at them without destroying them, the history is still just as lost."

"Funny, I said something similar when I first came here.

And now the civilization that destroyed my world is another fading memory to your kind."

"My kind, huh? In one breath you speak as though your human life matters, while in the next you talk as though we are entirely different species. Which is it?"

Arete smiled, shook her head, and offered no other answer. Instead she strolled over to a table and sat on its edge. "It'll be evening very soon. We are children of the night. Soon, Tanna will grow more active. Already, our servants whisper of his agents hunting you. If they do not know you are here, they soon will."

Efficient, but not really surprising. "We want to draw him out anyway. Maybe I should help the others get ready, though. If it's almost time ..."

"We have a little while yet." She cocked her head to the side. "Something strikes me, Starkad. You've had a long life. That much I could garner from your blood. Long for a human man, at least. A mere blink of the eye to an immortal."

"So?"

"So, what if it could be so very much longer? Indefinite, even?"

Damn. She meant if he became like her. Deathless, but not really alive either. Starkad shook his head. "Not sure I'd want to live forever."

"What?" Arete made no effort to cover the shock on her face. "Why ever not? Do not tell me you truly believe human fancies about some glorious afterlife awaiting those who live and die well? As a being who has seen the dark of the Otherworlds, I assure you, naught better than this life awaits you beyond."

Now there was a sobering thought. The brutal, bloody, merciless world of men was as good as it got? Starkad shook his head. "Long life has cost me rather much already. Prices I paid willingly, without really understanding their weight. Things I'd have to carry with me down through the years. I walked away from immortality once already."

Arete rocked back as if uncertain whether to ask what he meant. She apparently decided against that, because she hopped off the table. "Then maybe it is time for you to get your people ready for the attack. We leave in an hour."

Starkad stared at her as she left. A strange creature, for certain. She'd drank his blood when torturing him. A day later, she was—apparently—offering him immortality. Why? Did she truly taste something so very tempting inside him?

It hardly mattered. At least he kept trying to tell himself that. But her words had rent something open in him. Something that had to wonder if maybe some part of what she'd said about his need to wander might be the truth.

If maybe he'd been searching for something all this time. Something that dwelt here in Miklagard.

※

IN THE MAIN HALL, Starkad found Hervor grunting as she tried to wriggle on her mail. All their gear, weapons, and armor lay in a pile on the floor, apparently returned to them. Starkad strode toward Hervor and helped her ease into the armor.

"Shoulder acting up?"

"They had me hanging by my arms."

"Me too." Brought back visions of being tortured in the Otherworlds, in fact, though he had no desire to speak of it.

"And the bitch bit me."

"Yeah."

"That's it?" Hervor demanded. "Yeah?" She jerked her mail down then stepped back to glare at him. "So we're not even going to discuss her coming out of your room, face glowing like she'd had the best fuck of her immortal life?"

He flinched. "Have I given you reason to mistrust me?"

"No!" she snapped, like that alone was enough reason to be angry with him. She groaned. "No. But I hate this city and I tire of watching the people around me eviscerated by horrors most people cannot even imagine."

Starkad scratched his beard. "What are you saying?"

"I'm saying this plan is mist-madness. Tanna tore through us once already, and then he didn't know we were coming. Now he might be suspecting us."

"No. Not inside his own palace, not until it's too late. Besides, he surprised us, too. None of us were prepared to face a creature of such speed or ferocity. Now we are."

Afrid snorted behind him. "We shouldn't be doing this. We should be looking for a way out of Miklagard."

Starkad spun on her, stared hard until the other shield-maiden looked away. "Maybe you weren't paying attention, but I gave my oath. In blood. I do not break my vows."

"She's just scared," Veborg said. The varulf hadn't bothered with armor. In fact, she wore a robe like Nikolaos's, maybe for the ease of shedding it so she could shift. For all Starkad knew, the varulf could smell fear.

And he didn't blame them for being scared. None of them. But it was what it was. "Look, none of us knew what we were getting into when this started. But we're here now, and the only way out is through."

Win was leaning against one of the columns, arms folded, staring at Starkad. "You have something to add, prince?"

"Just that Tanna killed people we cared about, we loved.

136

It's true most of all for Baruch and myself, but true regardless. Honor demands we avenge them."

Hervor flinched. Maybe as scared as Afrid. Starkad knew neither of them were cravens. He wanted to tell Hervor they'd been through worse, but he wasn't sure that was true. Of all the Otherworldly threats he'd overcome, none matched the speed, strength, and ferocity of these vampires.

Arete seemed to materialize out of the shadows by a column. "It's time. We'll go by way of the undercity."

Starkad nodded. "Lead the way."

THE TUNNELS beneath Miklagard must've stretched on for hundreds of miles, if not more. They seemed nigh to endless, in fact, though Arete seemed to know where she was bound. She kept a half step ahead of Starkad, guiding him, with the others behind. She didn't have a torch—nor seemed to need much light—so he held one. Him and several others behind him.

Hervor and Win were next in the line, the two of them muttering about what an abominable place Miklagard was. Much as Win's blind faith in the Aesir irked Starkad, the prince had seemed almost broken by Nikolaos's claims that Odin had been here not long before and limped away like a whipped hound.

Nor was Starkad quite certain what to make of such a tale. The way the Patriarch told it lent credence to the story. Maybe that was how Odin had sent those cryptic warnings to Starkad about this place. If so, it would've been rather opportune had Odin bothered to explain in a hair more detail just what Starkad was walking into. Indeed, had the

Ás king lured Starkad here directly in the hopes of reclaiming Mistilteinn for the North Realms?

That much seemed quite likely.

So, then, if he was to believe the Patriarch, Odin had come to Miklagard and barely survived. The man had angered the Patriarchs, but not enough that any of them launched a war against Odin's followers. Odin, possibly reeling, had next guided Starkad here. Had made a nominal attempt to warn him about the vampires, but couldn't or wasn't willing to offer details.

Starkad had to believe Odin wanted him to succeed in claiming the runeblade. So why hadn't the Ás done more to ensure that happened? The man may not have been a god— not the way Win and Hervor thought—but his motivations were nigh as unfathomable as a true being of the Otherworlds.

"Reckon this might even be worse than Pohjola." Höfund said. The big man was the only one who seemed little unnerved by Vebiorg, so the two of them were talking together. "Can't say as I've ever smelt worse than this, me."

"Imagine how it smells to a wolf."

"Huh. Worse than to the rest of us, I reckon."

Arete fell back beside him and leaned in close. "Your companions are colorful. Vibrant, even. But are they really your equal? Are they the kind you will be happy spending long years beside?"

"Some of them." Could Hervor hear Arete? The shield-maiden seemed deep in her grumblings with Win. A small blessing, honestly. The last thing he needed now was her taking offense—justified offense—at Arete's attempt to undermine her.

"Truly?" Arete asked, as if genuinely shocked at his response. She pointed to a side tunnel. "We must pass through a section of the sewers, I'm afraid." The vampire stepped up onto the wall, deftly avoiding walking through the muck.

Starkad glowered. No one else in their party would be half so fortunate, of course. No, best to get it over with, though. He hopped down in the filth that splashed up on his shins before settling back down around his ankles.

"Oh, Odin's lumpy stones, Starkad!"

He didn't glance back at Hervor, not wanting her to see his grin. Sometimes her reactions alone made a hardship worthwhile. How strange, really, to have so many men swearing by the name of a man he'd met. Starkad remembered when Odin had been chosen as King of the Aesir, back before most of them had even heard of Idunn or Yggdrasil or imagined men could become immortal.

How different his life might've been had he stayed among them. He'd given up immortality because of Vikar and grew to resent him for it. And now he was giving up a second chance at it for Hervor. He swore to himself he'd never resent her for that, though. He was making his own choices.

Behind him, his companions sloshed through the dank tunnel. Even the banter had died down. Perhaps opening their mouths to talk while wading through shit stretched even their natures beyond the breaking points. Starkad did not mind the silence.

It gave him time to think, though, which could prove dangerous. Hervor had made it clear she wanted him to give up his wanderings. Having tried—repeatedly—he knew himself well enough to know that wouldn't take. Maybe Arete had spoken the truth in supposing that was less a curse and more his own nature being dissatisfied with what he'd gotten out of life since leaving the Aesir.

But if so, that was a bitter draught and he'd prefer not to swallow it.

He was making his own godsdamned choices. And if it so mattered to Hervor, he'd make another go at sticking in one place. Maybe they could make a home for themselves, even if he could never give her children.

"We're nearly there," Arete said after a long stretch of silence. She stepped off the wall and onto another mostly dry surface, leading them through a tunnel. Eventually, she paused at a ladder on the side of the wall. "Tanna's palace will have wards of its own. They prevent me from entering without his permission. But you, humans, will be unaffected."

"What about me?" Vebiorg asked.

Arete sneered. "I doubt a Patriarch concerns himself with dogs."

Vebiorg cast a vicious smile back at the vampire, shoved her aside, and grabbed the ladder. She stopped, though, looking at the trapdoor. "Is this one going to be locked, too?"

"Surely even a dog can break a lock."

"No, wait," Baruch said. "Let me try picking it. Less noisy."

Arete chuckled. "A thief. How wonderful, dear Starkad. You truly do have an interesting team on your hands."

Starkad glared at her. She was not making this any easier.

Baruch climbed the ladder, fiddled with the trapdoor, then eased it open. The Miklagardian slipped into a room above, then beckoned the others to follow.

Vebiorg surged up the ladder before Starkad could even move. Despite himself, he was almost glad she was here. And on their side.

He climbed up next. The room inside was not dissimilar

to the one they'd entered Nikolaos's palace from. A blood circle painted with runes ringed the trapdoor, and various crates lined the walls. A storeroom. And they could only assume that, like Nikolaos, Tanna would have his own guards just outside to deal with intruders.

Hervor followed him up, and he grabbed her hand to help her crest the ridge. Win came next, and finally Höfund. Starkad looked over his crew, then down the hatch. Arete had already vanished into the darkness, perhaps intent to report back to Nikolaos. He'd made clear he couldn't have this traced back to him, whatever doubt his actions might have cast upon him. She probably had orders not to stay too close.

"All right," he said. "We don't know how many vampires may lair in here. So we need to go in quiet. If we're discovered, we lose the element of surprise."

Afrid whimpered, mumbling something to herself. Starkad had no time to coddle her. Arete had provided her with a new spear. That had to be enough for her.

"Let me go first, then," Vebiorg said. "I've got the best senses and I'm good at being silent."

"Fine. Do it. Let's go."

The varulf slipped over to the door, then eased it open. Then she disappeared down a dimly lit hall. Starkad stalked after her, keeping low, keeping his footfalls light. No guards after all. Maybe Tanna only worried about vampire intruders.

The hallway let out into a large foyer broken up by twin winding staircases leading to a higher floor. The whole room was completely empty still.

Vebiorg glanced back at Starkad.

So which way would they find Tanna? Upstairs, probably. He pointed to the nearest of the staircases. The varulf stalked over to it and started up, Starkad a few steps behind her.

A shadow dropped down from above, in the corner of his eye, like it had fallen from the balcony. He turned, only to see six vampires had leapt down into the foyer, landing amid his crew, more than half of them coming down in his blind spot.

How the fuck had they known?

Afrid ran and ducked behind the stairs. Damn it, he knew he shouldn't have brought someone so young on this mission.

Höfund, flailing with his great axe, charged straight for a vampire. The creature moved so fast it almost seemed a blur as it dodged behind him, then brought a warhammer crashing down on the half-jotunn's back.

Shit. Starkad didn't have time to save them all.

He leapt over the side of the banister, drawing his swords all in one motion and whipping them in a cross as he fell. His blades sunk into a vampire below him, drawing forth spurts of blood and sending the creature shrieking like the damned from the gates of Hel.

"I'm sorry!" Afrid wailed. Starkad spun to see the shield-maiden run toward one of the vampires. The creature jerked the shieldmaiden behind himself and advanced on Starkad. Over its shoulder, Starkad gaped at Afrid. "I just ... just didn't want to die!"

One of the other vampires had Baruch pinned the opposite staircase. He screamed as it bit down on his throat. The vampire jerked its head back, ripping out Baruch's jugular in the process and spraying a shower of blood across the marble floor.

Hervor shrieked, sunk Tyrfing into a vampire up to the

hilt. The creature writhed as the runeblade's pale flames scorched it. She had it well in hand.

Starkad had to see to this one. The creature lunged at him, a knife in each hand. He parried one, dodged the other and cut with his second sword. But the vampire had inhuman speed and much lighter weapons. They set about their dance, and it was all he could do to keep up. His swords gave him reach, but it amounted to little when the vampire didn't fear minor wounds. Naught much seemed to faze it, in truth.

More vampires were pouring into the foyer. This was all a fucking trap. This had all gone wrong. "Flee!" he shouted. "Back to the tunnels, flee!"

At his words, Hervor jerked Tyrfing free of her foe, spun around and lopped its head off. Starkad didn't even have time to marvel at her move, so pressed by the vampire. Instead, he gave ground willingly, retreating back toward the same hallway they'd come from.

"I'm sorry," Afrid shouted again, from somewhere beyond the stairs. Starkad had no time to think on her.

An awful grunt escaped Höfund, followed by a crash to the floor, but Starkad couldn't see him.

Hervor raced to Starkad's side, then past him, maybe helping one of the others. Starkad kept giving ground to the knife-wielder, until he came back to the hall. He needed just a slight chance to break off and run, but this vampire wasn't giving—

A wolf flew through the air, tackled the vampire, and bit down on its throat. Snarling, growling. Rending flesh. Vebiorg jerked away and dashed down the hall. Starkad needed no invitation to follow.

Hervor and Win were already back in the cellar, engaged

with human guards. Hervor cleaved into one and Win felled the other.

"Jump!" Starkad bellowed. "The tunnels!"

Vebiorg snapped at something, but he had no chance to see what. He raced to the trapdoor, dropped down, and slid to the edge. Then he dropped down into the darkness.

## 20

*O*din's stones! Hervor dashed blindly down another tunnel, took the next bend, and took off running again, her feet squelching in Odin-knew-what.

"Do you even know where you're going?" Win shouted, a half step behind her.

"No!"

"Then how do you know we do not run in circles?"

Hervor didn't even bother to answer that. The vampires were much faster than humans. She needed to keep changing directions until she was certain they'd lost their pursuit. Naught else really mattered. If they did wind up going in a circle ... they were probably all dead.

She'd lost track of Vebiorg. Could only pray Starkad was back behind Win, following. Everything had turned to troll shit. Afrid ... Hel take that bitch. Hervor had believed in her, liked her. And she'd betrayed them.

Hervor's chest hurt from sucking in heaving breath after breath. Made it hard to think clear. To understand *why* Stonekicker would do it. Fucking craven.

Hervor's foot skidded on sludge and she blundered into the tunnel wall.

Win caught her, kept her from toppling over into the muck. "I don't think this is the way back to Nikolaos's estate."

Hervor didn't fucking care, so long as they got away from Tanna's palace.

"This seems almost like we've wandered into an actual maze."

"I agree," Starkad answered, trotting up behind them. "And I barely managed to find you. Without Arete or Vebiorg, we're wandering blind down here."

Hervor spun on him. "They got Höfund!"

"I know."

"This is on you, Starkad. You brought us here, and now one of our crew is in Tanna's hands."

Win held up his hands. "We don't have time to cast blame upon one another. If this place is a deliberate maze beneath Tanna's holdings, we need to focus our efforts on finding egress."

Starkad grimaced. "I might ... I have good instincts. I may be able to find a way through."

"Instincts?" Hervor asked. "Did they warn you about Afrid?"

He winced. Maybe he didn't deserve it. But who else was she to blame?

"Shit," she mumbled. "We can't go forward. We *have* to go back for Höfund."

Starkad flinched and stared at her with sad eyes.

Win was already shaking his head. "We do him no good by sacrificing our lives in a vain attempt to reach him. Tanna's minions already caught us unawares and handily defeated us. Our numbers are fewer now." The prince left the mention of Baruch unspoken.

The Miklagardian had died for this mission. He'd escaped this city long ago, earned his way free from slavery, made a life for himself. Since coming back here, he'd lost Fjolvor and then his own life.

"Stonekicker has betrayed us," Win finally said. "Vebiorg is missing. Höfund is captured. Are the three of us to do what seven failed to?"

"We'll find a way to go back for him," Starkad said. "Not now, though. Right now, we need to get free of this place. The only way I can see to do that is to press on and try to navigate this maze of tunnels."

And Hel take them both for being right. Why the fuck did Höfund have to throw in his lot with Rollaugr? And the big man had trusted her and Starkad to help solve this. She'd failed him, every way a friend could. When she'd asked for his help to save Starkad from the witches of Pohjola, Höfund had come running. And this was how she repaid him.

"Lead the way, then," she snapped at Starkad.

He did, heading out a few steps ahead of them. He paused at an intersection. Thinking? Or ... Oh. Odin's bleeding stones. He was trying to use the Sight to get Otherworldly guidance. Even the thought of it had the hair on Hervor's arms standing on end. Maybe that insight had helped them a time or two. Still, it seemed a fell, even fey gift—or a curse. She couldn't help but mistrust aught that didn't come from the human world. More so now, given all she'd seen in the past seven years.

Starkad led them down bend after bend. Maybe the Sight told him where to go. Maybe he just wandered nigh as blind as she had, but didn't admit it. Didn't want them scared any worse than they already were. He needn't have bothered if that was the case. She couldn't have gotten much more scared.

Down the next tunnel, the sound of metal scraping over stone reached her. What now?

Even Starkad glanced back at her, a hint of concern on his face. "I'm fair certain we need to continue this way."

"Then let us do so," Win said.

With a nod, Starkad pressed on. They came round a bend and the source of the sound became clear, if hard to believe. Great sweeping blades the size of a man flashed out of grooves in the walls, cutting across the hall in an arc one way. Then the other.

Behind them, the sound of grinding stone echoed through the tunnel.

"Not this way," Hervor said.

"I'd say not," Win agreed.

Starkad frowned. "Who would build this?"

Tanna probably, though Hervor didn't much care, truth be told. She spun around and doubled back. Only ... hadn't the bend been to the left when they'd come around? No, she must just be exhausted. It was right.

Beside her, Win was blinking, shaking his head.

Whatever. Hervor started down the tunnel. That grinding sound just kept going and going, like a mill inside her head. There was another intersection, with a way to her left and a way straight on.

As she approached, a section of the wall maybe five feet on a side began to shift over the floor, grinding, closing off the intersection. She spun around, gaping, finding Starkad and Win doing much the same.

"How ...?" she mumbled. How and why would anyone build something like this? It made no sense.

"These vampires predate even the Old Kingdoms," Win said. "Perhaps they know secrets long forgotten by the world."

Even if that explained the how, it hardly said much about the why.

Starkad swept his torch close to the wall that had closed off that intersection.

"Are we being herded?" Hervor asked.

He was still inspecting the now-flush block. "I'm not sure. I suspect all this was designed to confuse as much as herd. Given centuries ... millennia, even, with which to work, the vampires must've designed this place to hinder their own kind as much as humans."

"So what do we do?" she demanded.

"Naught has changed save that we could not go back even if we wished to do so. We must press forward and seek another escape from the undercity."

Hervor grimaced. An awful, sick realization settled on her gut. They were going to die. Despite all they'd survived, her and Starkad, all they'd been through, they were over-matched this time. Facing foes they barely understood. Caught in a game where they didn't fathom the rules. And they'd been defeated at every turn.

So then, it was only a matter of time before Tanna or some other vampire cornered them and killed them. And she couldn't think of a damn thing she could do to change that.

## 21

"How did you know where they'd be?" Orvar asked Tanna as the vampire Patriarch led him to a dungeon beneath the palace. This far down, they had to be adjacent to the sewer system Hervor and the others had fled into.

Tanna chuckled ever so slightly. "Ah. A particular gift of mine. If a human willingly surrenders his—or her—soul to me, I can see through her eyes."

Tanna's agent among Hervor's crew. "Who was it?"

"A girl, really. A child among them I cornered when they first attacked my tower. She begged for her life. So I gave it to her. After tasting her blood, of course, and binding her to me. Maybe I'll even make her one of us, someday."

They entered a corridor lit by small torches stuck in sconces, with steel doors every so often. Tanna bypassed several such doors before pausing at one. He twisted his hand oddly and something clicked. Then the door popped open on its own.

Orvar raised an eyebrow but said naught. He caught the edge of the door and flung it the rest of the way open.

Inside, the vampires had chained up the big man who'd been working with Hervor. Bigger even than Ecgtheow had been, in fact—Orvar sometimes wondered what happened to him.

If some fell urd, he deserved it. He too had been on the crew on Thule. The ones who had abandoned Orvar.

*Vengeance. Vengeance. Vengeance.*

This other man might've been half jotunn, actually.

"Did you know," Tanna said, drawing a small vial from beneath his robes, "we studied a concoction those fire-worshipping Serklanders developed? We developed our own formula for it, one which we use in large quantities to repel any attempt at naval invasion. This small quantity of it has other amusing uses, though."

The vampire handed Orvar the vial.

Orvar uncorked it. It just smelled like oil to him. Looked like it, too. "What do I care of it?"

"Liquid fire, my friend. Water will only make it spread. It just burns and burns ..." Tanna cocked his head toward the big man chained to the wall. "I must see to the other inter-lopers. One of them carries a runeblade I intend to claim."

Hervor herself, in fact.

"Amuse yourself with the oaf and learn what you can. When you're finished with him, tell Nilos and he'll have you brought to me. I wouldn't want you to miss the end."

No. Orvar definitely wouldn't want to miss that.

*Vengeance. Vengeance. Vengeance.*

Tanna strode back down the hall they'd come from, leaving Orvar alone with the big man.

He drifted into the room and paced around. Tanna's people had manacled Hervor's companion's hands behind his back, with those manacles then chained to the floor.

"Reckon you're the one, ain't you?"

Orvar cocked his head at the man's words. "She *told* you?" As far as he'd known, Hervor had gone to substantial lengths to keep anyone from learning of her crime of betraying and murdering him. How important this man must be to her, if she trusted him with such dangerous knowledge.

The big man shrugged, jiggling the chains in the process. "Gonna have to kill you eventually. Just being upfront about that."

Orvar chuckled, a sound that made the big man recoil. His laughter had that effect on the living now. It sounded hollow, Otherworldly. Perils of being among the damned. "Who are you?"

"Höfund Godmundson. You?"

Good question. "Once, Orvar-Oddr Grimrson. Later, they called me the Arrow's Point. There was a time I thought I left even that name behind. Now, I am dead. So perhaps I am Orvar, or perhaps something else."

"Huh. Kinda overlong answer to a simple question. Like to hear yourself talk?"

Orvar frowned. Then he caught Höfund with a hook to the face. His blow sent blood and spittle flying. A moment later, the man spit out two teeth.

"Did you know I had a half-jotunn son?" Orvar shook his head at the thought. "I passed into Jotunheim once, and lay with a jotunn woman." His son had been big like Höfund, but with an easy smile. "I dare not even show myself to him now. Not after what Hervor made me into."

Höfund spit out more blood. "Reckon maybe you deserved it. Either way, most people what pick up a sword or axe or spear got some blood on their hands. Children and farmers might get the chance of being good. Maybe. Not even sure on that account. Warriors, we got different rules."

"Indeed." Orvar punched him in the face again, twice. Then he landed a blow to the man's gut. That one sent the half-jotunn retching up blood and everything else in his stomach. Orvar landed another hook to the man's left ribs with a satisfying crack. Two broken, if he made his guess. With his other hand he punched Höfund's right side, cracking another rib.

The big man dropped to his knees, hacking and coughing, sputtering up more blood.

*Vengeance. Vengeance. Vengeance.*

"Rules," Orvar muttered. "Blood for blood. The evil bitch murdered me and must reap her reward."

Inexplicably, Höfund laughed between coughing fits, blood soaking his teeth and dribbling down his chin. "Evil? Ain't any such thing so far as I've seen. There's just the people what you care about, and the people what you don't." He wheezed again, obviously pained to draw breath. "Your way'd leave all Midgard bloody."

Utter drivel. Orvar knelt down, bringing the man's face level with his own. "Death provides one clarity of thought and purpose the living could not fathom. Blood is everything. You do not understand. But you soon will. When your soul is cast into the void to drown in eternal torment beyond this life, then you will know I have told you the truth."

"Could be. Or could be you're just fucking mist-mad and can't tell your mouth from your arse. Reckon 'cause you've got vampire cocks stuck in both."

Orvar seized the half-jotunn by the throat and squeezed. Hervor cared for this man on some level, valued him, at least as much as the self-absorbed bitch could value the life of another. His death would hurt her, maybe have slightly more effect than all the others.

Then again, maybe making her watch the big man draw his last dying gasp would be sweeter.

*Vengeance. Vengeance. Vengeance.*

Orvar released the big man. He drew the vial Tanna had given him from his shirt, then upended it over Höfund's feet. Naught happened. Maybe, like oil, it needed a spark.

After grabbing a torch, Orvar tossed it at the big man's boots. His screams of agony caught even Orvar off guard and sent him falling back several steps. The acrid stench of burning flesh filled the room. He chuckled, shaking his head. What foulness these Miklagardians had come up with. As if men did not have enough awful ways of killing one another.

In truth, though, he hoped the fires wouldn't kill the half-jotunn. Hervor should see his end, just before her own.

So then, time to find Nilos, and then Hervor. The time had come to crush her out of existence at long last.

## 22

endulum blades swung back and forth across the tunnel. Starkad frowned, judging the timing. They could double back once more, of course. Could take their chances wandering around this maze longer.

But they'd seen shifting blocks closing off passageways and fires that somehow never seemed to burn out. And more blades like these, making every corridor its own deathtrap.

It had been hours already, and the constantly shifting passageways had done naught but delay them and cut off any attempt at return. While he knew no conscious mind ran this maze, still he could not help but feel someone was toying with him.

Urd, maybe.

Either way, sooner or later, they would have to stop turning away from the traps and cross one.

"What are you doing?" Hervor asked. "There's another tunnel behind us."

"It goes nowhere."

155

"You don't know that."

His instincts insisted that way would only send them wandering deeper into the convoluted paths. He shook his head. "We can do this."

"You jest," Win said. "Those blades are the bigger than even Höfund's axe. I hope you do not think your mail will protect you if one catches you."

"No. I'm going to avoid getting hit. Wait for it to pass, step forward, wait for the next, and so on."

The prince groaned. "This is not some child's game of balancing on logs over the river."

Starkad spun on him. "None of this is a fucking game. People are dead and my goal here is to keep from losing any more of the crew. Every moment we delay may bring the vampires closer toward us. If we can make it to the upper city, if we can survive until daylight, maybe we have a chance. But down here, the sun never comes up, and we cannot afford to be caught out."

Hervor was staring at him, face grim. Clearly, she knew he had the right of it, because she pushed past him to pause just before the first of the three pendulums. As it swung back the other way she lurched forward, then pulled up just short of the next. She repeated the maneuver twice more to come out on the other side.

Starkad looked to Win. "You see what she did? I'm going to repeat it. Just learn the timing, same as you'd study a foe in a duel, except these blades never vary their speed. You're dodging an axe blow. No more or less than that."

So, then. Starkad watched the blades, danced forward when one passed, and then repeated it twice more to join Hervor.

He glanced back at Win. "Come on."

"Starkad," Hervor said. She was looking down the

tunnel, into a circle chamber with other paths branching off it like rays of the sun. And striding down one of them, runeblade in hand, was Tanna.

Alone. Supremely confident.

Growling, Hervor drew Tyrfing. Pale flames sprang to life along the blade's length. The shieldmaiden stalked forward.

"Hurry up, Win!" Starkad shouted, pulling his own swords. He raced to catch up to Hervor.

"It's two on one," she said. "We can do this."

Starkad wanted to believe that. But Tanna's speed was almost unfathomable. His strength like that of a troll.

The vampire bared his fangs, uttering a hissing growl. He lunged forward without further warning, his form blurring, becoming half a dust cloud as he flew at them.

Starkad shoved Hervor to one side with his elbow and then swung both swords at Tanna. In a blur, the vampire parried one blade and jerked Mistilteinn up to knock aside the other. And then Starkad was the one on the defensive, desperately parrying and ducking Tanna's blindingly fast assault.

Roaring, Hervor came in, cleaving with Tyrfing. The vampire's form became dust and then solidified, facing Hervor and bringing Mistilteinn up to parry her blade. He kicked her in the gut, sending her flying through the air.

Hervor! Bellowing, Starkad thrust at Tanna. His form broke apart, letting the sword pass through harmlessly, before reappearing to Starkad's side. On pure instinct, Starkad flung himself away in a roll, barely clearing the space before Mistilteinn whistled overhead.

Tanna's body came apart again, and reformed in front of Starkad, chopping downward before he'd gained his feet. Starkad rolled to the side once more.

Win's broadsword cleaved into Tanna's shoulder, wedging down into his collarbone. The vampire bellowed in pain, an inhuman cry that echoed off the chamber and sent Starkad's brain recoiling.

Half crawling, half running, Starkad scrambled to where Hervor had fallen. The shieldmaiden had pushed herself up to her knees, hands around her gut, clearly trying to catch a breath.

Starkad let go of one of his swords and snatched up Tyrfing. Hervor would forgive him for that, eventually. The blade flared to life in his hand, filling with enhanced vigor. And rage.

Win lay collapsed on the floor, so Starkad could only guess at what had happened to him. Tanna had driven Mistilteinn into the stone. The vampire grabbed the broadsword wedged into his shoulder by the blade, ripped it free, and tossed it aside, spraying blood in the process.

Even as Starkad closed in on him, the vampire's wound began to close. That was fucking wonderful, wasn't it?

Hissing, the vampire lord jerked Mistilteinn up and focused on Starkad.

"I don't care how many centuries you've lived," Starkad said. "I'm going to kill you. I'll send your soul screaming down to Hel."

Tanna snickered. "How old am I ...? Old enough to know that dark goddess by other, older names."

"Well, then you two should have a lot to talk about. I imagine she'll be glad to see you." Starkad charged forward, leading with his normal sword.

Predictably, Tanna's body turned to dust and he flew around Starkad. Spinning around, Starkad whipped Tyrfing in an arc. The flaming runeblade cut through Tanna's gut even as the vampire tried to hack at Starkad. All strength left

Tanna's blow, and the vampire fell back, hand to his abdomen.

It came away bloody. This wound wasn't healing so quick, either.

Starkad bared his own teeth at Tanna. "I've slain alfar and draugar and dragons. You're just an old man who doesn't know when to die."

Tanna hissed at him, then exploded into lightning-fast attacks. Starkad parried one, then another, ducked, dodged. Tanna's form kept turning half to dust, leaving all of Starkad's blows empty.

The vampire's assault forced Starkad to give ground rapidly. It didn't seem that wound was going to kill him, was it? Did the poison not work on immortals? Win was groaning somewhere behind Starkad, alive but clearly in no shape to help.

At Hervor's war cry, though, Tanna spun, parrying a blow that would've split his skull. Hervor swung again, this time clearly trying to lop the vampire's head clean off.

Since Tanna knew that was the only way to kill him in one blow, he saw it coming. It made it too easy for him to dodge or parry or just break up his body into dust.

So Starkad didn't bother going for the head. He swung both swords at Tanna's legs. The vampire broke apart, but not before Starkad's ordinary blade nicked flesh. Tanna became a flurry of dust, breaking apart and re-forming facing in different directions, parrying and attacking so fast sometimes he looked like he was in more than one place at a time.

Damn it. Just fucking die! Starkad feinted one of his steel blades, then thrust with Tyrfing. The vampire broke apart to avoid the blow. Starkad jerked Tyrfing along through the dust cloud, guessing at what direction Tanna would try to flow.

His guess proved right, and Tanna re-formed with the flaming runeblade embedded in his gut. Bellowing, Starkad yanked it free.

Tanna was staring at him. Eyes wide with shock.

Yes. A man had beaten him. Yes, he was going to die.

Starkad swept Tyrfing back around, but Tanna broke apart once more. Starkad was expecting that too, and kept sweeping the blade around.

The dust cloud didn't re-form, though. Instead, it passed right through Hervor, sending her coughing and stumbling. Starkad pulled up short, not daring to risk hitting Hervor with Tyrfing. The cloud continued past her, flying down one of the tunnels faster than Starkad could've run.

"Fuck," he mumbled.

Hervor swept her hand in front of her face as if dust yet remained. Then she extended Starkad's other sword to him hilt-first while reaching out her hand for Tyrfing.

Always so attached to that runeblade. Whatever, Tanna was gone. Starkad handed over the blade, reclaiming his own. "I had hoped to claim Mistilteinn. I'm not sure how to corner him, unless we could draw him into the daylight."

"How are we to fight such an abomination?" Hervor demanded. "He lived through multiple wounds from Tyrfing!"

"I don't know. We'll figure something—"

"This is mist-madness!" Hervor shouted at him. "If we reach daylight, the only thing we ought to do is find a boat going anywhere but here."

Win coughed. "Much as I wished this mission to succeed, I fear I'm inclined to agree with the shieldmaiden.

We face a foe far beyond ourselves and possess no means of killing him."

Starkad spat. "I made an oath and I'm not giving it up."

A dark, hollow chuckle echoed from one of the other tunnels. "You two and your oaths."

Starkad spun. Another vampire? But that voice sounded inhuman, like a draug or other ghost.

He brought both swords up.

The creature that strode forward had red eyes that gleamed in the darkness, reflecting off the torch Starkad had dropped and the one Win had taken up. The draug drew closer, revealing its rotting flesh.

Starkad hadn't realized the vampires employed draugar. But just one here, and he should be able to handle it, even winded as he was.

"No, no, no," Hervor was mumbling.

The draug continued to advance, sword in hand but not even raised.

As Win came up behind Starkad, the torchlight fell upon the draug's face.

A face Starkad had known for years, though now it had turned rotten with decay. The face of a friend, long dead. A face that could not be here.

## 23

Orvar-Oddr, the Arrow's Point. For years he had tormented Hervor, a presence in the shadows. A whisper in the darkness, haunting her, always drawing out her torment. But never, in all that time, had he shown himself before her when others were about.

Eventually, Hervor had come to realize that had been its own little torment. Forcing her to live alone, to keep the truth of her crime buried, always fearing when it would come out.

Her gut clenched now, trying to rebel. Her heart felt apt to burst. Her right hand was twitching, a phantom pain in the finger the draug had bitten off long ago.

"Orvar?" Starkad asked, taking a half step toward. "Orvar? Oh ... my friend. I had not considered you would meet such a dark urd." He shook his head sadly. "We failed you, didn't we? Failed to give you a proper send-off. And I should've ... should've known."

Orvar chuckled. Fuck. Fuck him.

Hervor bellowed and charged the draug, Tyrfing flashing. The draug ducked out of the way, came up behind Hervor, and kicked her in the arse, sending her sprawling.

The draug snickered as Hervor struggled to her feet.

"Forgive me," Starkad said. "I cannot imagine how you've come here, but I will bring you the peace of oblivion you ought to have had these long years."

Win was circling the draug as Hervor regained her feet. They could do this together, maybe silence him before he could tell all.

"You still don't know," Orvar said.

Hervor shrieked and came in swinging, Tyrfing's blue flames crackling through the air. Orvar dodged, falling back from each, parrying only once. The impact numbed Hervor's arm and forced her to end her assault.

Win lunged in, hacked Orvar in the side with his broadsword. The effort earned him a cuff to the side of the head that sent him toppling to the ground, clearly dazed.

"Why would a draug come so very far?" Orvar asked.

Odin's bloated stones! Why wasn't Starkad attacking?

"Help us!" Hervor shrieked at her lover.

"Vengeance ..." Starkad said. "Draugar care only for revenge. Y-you blamed us ... Maybe not without cause."

Orvar snickered.

Hervor brought Tyrfing down with a mighty two-handed chop. Her foe twisted out of the way with shocking speed, caught the back of her mail with one hand, and flung her at Starkad's feet. The world spun around as she tumbled, everything hazy for a moment.

"Vengeance. Because the bitch ran me through with a runeblade."

Starkad took a step back. "The draug prince ..."

Troll shit. Hervor struggled to rise, but her limbs felt like jelly. Her hand closed around Tyrfing, and the blade brought her strength, helped clear the wool from her head.

"Oh ..." Orvar said. "Yes. We killed the draug prince, the shieldmaiden and I. And then, one oath fulfilled, she saw to the next. Drove the flaming sword through my lung, which even now wheezes, punctured and scorched. Almost a relief I no longer draw breath."

Starkad had turned, was staring down at Hervor, gaping, backing away, shaking his head.

Orvar chuckled again. "Funny. She told the half-jotunn but not you."

"You told Höfund?" Starkad's mouth hung open after that, eyes wide, like she'd killed his beloved.

Hervor pulled up to her knees. "Starkad ... you have to listen." Didn't quite have her breath. "There are things you ... don't understand."

"You murdered my friend ... You lied to me. Told us that ..." Still backing away.

"He murdered my father!"

Orvar had drifted back into the shadows near to one of the tunnels. "Oh, delicious ... And it makes one wonder ... Ecgtheow disappeared not so long after I told him the truth."

Starkad blanched. "Ecgtheow? You ... you didn't ..."

Oh, Hel fucking take Orvar. "Starkad." Hervor gained her feet. "He's a draug. Otherworldly, made of lies. He's twisting the truth around, trying to drive us apart."

"He was my friend for years ... And Ecgtheow ... And you *lied* to me. You murdered those I cared about and lied about it. For years and years." His breaths were coming so fast he seemed like to faint from it. "You ... shared my bed ... I trusted you ... I trusted ... shouldn't have trusted a woman. I *knew* better."

Not this shit again. "Fuck you with that 'women are liars' shit, Starkad. You want the truth? I am the granddaughter of Arngrim the Berserk. I hunted the Arrow's Point for the murder of my family and I avenged them, as I'd given my oath to do so. You'd not have done less."

"I'd not have lied about it!"

"Arngrim ..." Win said. "Arngrim who ... The sword. Sigrlami's magic sword. The one ... you carry."

Hervor ignored the prince. "You know I speak the truth now. You must understand why I couldn't tell you."

"Yes ... because Orvar is right. You are a murderer, a betrayer. And you betrayed my trust!" Starkad took a step toward her now, swords raised before him. "You ... defiled me. Your treachery sickens me, even as I deserved it for my own crimes."

She hefted Tyrfing. "What're you doing? Starkad! Don't do this."

"There is naught left but *this*. You brought us here. Or urd did. Vengeance, upon me, for betraying my brother so long ago. I deserved it ... as urd must now guide *my* actions. Vengeance, your war cry, must be the last sound you hear."

Odin's stones! He'd lost his godsdamned mind. Gasping with short, shallow breaths, Hervor looked around. Orvar had disappeared into the shadows. Win was backing away from her, shaking his head in shock or loathing. And Starkad was closing in, seeming fey, almost possessed.

Without further warning, Starkad launched himself at her. His blades flashed in a terrible blur of death. Hervor ducked one, used Tyrfing to parry another, and dodged as the first blade came round again. It still caught her cheek, tearing open a gouge as long as her finger. The other came back around, hit her in the ribs and sent her reeling.

She barely got Tyrfing up to parry a sword coming down

to split her skull. Starkad's boot caught her thigh and sent her down to one knee.

Shrieking, desperate, she swung Tyrfing at Starkad's gut. He twisted away, using one blade to knock her attack wide.

Rising and using her momentum, she swung not at him, but at the blade. Tyrfing flashed, chipped Starkad's sword and tore a shard from it. The metal piece flew past her face, a hair from embedding in her skull.

Starkad gaped at his sword, grimaced, and tossed it aside.

By now, Hervor had backed away, putting space between them. She used her second hand to steady Tyrfing, to give it power. Maybe she couldn't match Starkad's speed or skill, but she wasn't dying without a fight. If the bastard refused to see her side of it, that was on him.

She whipped Tyrfing around in an arc, hoping to keep Starkad at bay. "We don't have to do this."

"Urd brought us invariably here." Starkad stalked forward, his own blade now steadied with his other hand, mirroring her posture. "It demanded this from us. The strands of fate bound us to this end, maybe from before either of us was even born. I tried ... to think I could master urd. But it held me in its grasp, just as Odin promised. I denied him, like a fool."

"You sound like one now." Urd was one thing, but Starkad wasn't making any sense. "We still have choices."

He roared, coming in with rapid swings, though the fatigue had slowed him a bit. Hervor concentrated only on parrying. Tyrfing gave her additional stamina to carry on where she otherwise might have faltered. She had to count on that now.

Orvar's maddening cackles echoed around the room, interspersed by the clang of metal on metal and the heavy panting coming from her and Starkad. Again and again his blade passed a hairsbreadth from her flesh. A fell rage had taken him, a madness Orvar had engendered in him.

And she had lost him.

The thought—the utter certainty—hit her like a blow from a jotunn's club. It hammered her mind down into pitiful numbness, unable to form a thought, even as her body continued to fight on reflex. A numbness and a rage of her own. Burning, searing at what she had lost.

At a future turned to ash by the Arrow's Point.

At her worst fear come to light.

Shrieking, she whipped Tyrfing up to parry. The runeblade tore through Starkad's other sword and continued up, cleaving into his chin and out the front of his mouth.

He toppled backward, moaning and clutching a hand to the spot where she'd half severed his jaw. He was on the ground, writhing.

Dying.

Tyrfing's poison would do its work.

No.

No.

Fucking no!

Orvar's hysterical cackles now drowned out even the sound of Starkad's whimpers of pain. Odin's ... Oh ... gods ... what had she done?

She stared aghast at Tyrfing, blood trickling down into its runes. It demanded blood. Always, always blood. Never sated.

Starkad fell to his back, thrashed. Convulsed. Poisoned ...

Oh fuck ... oh gods no ...

Hervor backed away, unable to bear the horrid sight of

what she'd done. Her lover ... her beloved ... her future ... dying.

"Hel take you all!" she shrieked and flung Tyrfing to the floor. It slid along the stone, flames winking out.

Urd ... he had said.

Urd.

The fate of the damned. Like her. Like them all. Damned, all along.

Unable to still her frantic breaths, Hervor fled down the nearest tunnel.

Damned, because hope had always been a lie.

# PART III

Eleventh Moon
Year 31, Age of the Aesir

## 24

*R*ivers of agony surged through Starkad's veins as he writhed on the floor, unable to still the convulsions even as he cracked his skull on the stone over and over. The runeblade's poison arced through him in burning pulses.

It ought to have killed him by now.

Like in the Otherworlds. He'd wanted to die. Ought to have died, over and over.

His tremors eased just enough that he managed a feeble groan. A gasp of pain.

An agonizing, failed attempt to roll over onto his side. Followed by more wretched, burning breaths.

The dim awareness that blood was oozing from his split jaw. That the bone hung loose, half-severed on one side.

A figure crouched over him. Rotting, as dead as Starkad soon should be. Almost as dead. Orvar-Oddr. A fallen friend ... "You're dying, Eightarms. Slowly, in agony, poisoned by both the runeblade and its viperous owner."

All Starkad could do was grunt. Any attempt to move his jaw resulted in fresh bouts of blinding pain.

"She sunk her fangs into you, didn't she? Filled you with her venom, her lies. Poison that you swallowed for years ..." Orvar shook his head. "The dead are not known for their mercy. I hated you. All of you who left me. Those who sent me in the first place. Everyone left alive. I hate you all. But, almost, I pity you, Eightarms. Once the most glorious, famed warrior in the North Realms."

Starkad groaned.

Orvar chuckled his hateful laugh once more. "What are you now? More than half blind? Maimed? Even if you weren't poisoned, it seems you would never speak again. Maybe never eat solid food. Did she bring you to this end? Or perhaps, as you supposed, it was all urd." He snickered at some private joke Starkad had neither the time nor the strength for. "In the name of old friends, I offer you one gift. To end this swiftly for you. I can tear out your throat and be done with it."

Done with it all ... Done with the suffering and lies and betrayals and constant disappointments. Maybe, in the Otherworlds, part of him had longed for that. It had been what Ogn had wanted, of course. To see him give up and lose himself.

But Starkad wasn't the giving up type. Maybe that was urd, too.

Snarling, he shook his head, as much as his wounds allowed at any rate.

Orvar chuckled again. "Then die in agony or live in worse if you somehow manage it. Either way, we heap suffering on the one who brought us here." He rose, baring fang-like teeth. "Speaking of her, it's time for me to go and put an end to this. How far do you think she made it?"

Without another look, Orvar rose and strode down one of the tunnels, leaving Starkad alone in the chamber.

The only sound was the fading crackle of Starkad's torch and his own moans of torment.

❧

IT TOOK all he had to pull himself up to his feet. The suffering Tyrfing had wrought inside him had dimmed, casting the pain in his jaw into even starker relief.

Torch in one hand, the other supporting himself on the grimy wall, he limped and plodded down one of the tunnels. Didn't matter which, other than that it wasn't the one Hervor and Orvar had gone down.

He had no idea what had become of Win, save that the prince appeared to have taken Tyrfing, since both were missing and he didn't recall Orvar claiming the runeblade.

He couldn't bring himself to much care anymore.

*I swear to stay by your side, then. I give you my oath of love, Hervor. I swear it! I swear it!*

He'd given Hervor his oath ... And she'd forced him to become an oathbreaker. And herself in the process.

Maybe Odin's spell prevented Tyrfing from quite killing him. The runeblade had ravaged him, though. Torn through him like a blistering scythe, slicing and burning and destroying. He'd felt it, carving up his insides and leaving him hollow and pitiful. A shell of what he'd been. A shell of a man.

It felt like his jaw would just fall off any moment now. Would he die of *that*? He'd surely be praying for it if he had the slightest inclination to believe Odin would hear his prayer or, if he did, be able to do aught for Starkad. But Odin wouldn't do troll shit, wherever the fuck he was. He'd failed to warn Starkad about Miklagard and failed to warn him about Hervor.

Or maybe it was unfair to lay the blame for the last on the Ás. Starkad had mistrusted Hervor when he thought her a man and mistrusted her twice over when he learned she'd lied about that. And somehow, along the way, he'd let the mistrust slip.

*I give you my oath of love, Hervor. I swear it! I swear it!*

Starkad was a fool. Almost the same trap he'd fallen into with Ogn, and this one more painful somehow. This time, a betrayal years in the making. Years he had stayed by her side. Allowed himself to believe that, despite his curse, he might yet have a life for himself. Might have ... love.

Hel, for so long he'd been afraid of the very godsdamned word.

Rightly so, it seemed.

Each step only served to refresh the pain jolting up his body. The hideous torment in his jaw. The growing weakness as his blood seeped away. So in the end, he would die down here in the sewers, alone and damned.

Orvar had not been far off the mark in that guess.

*I swear to stay by your side, then.*

Starkad growled, the effort of it sending a fresh stream of blood gurgling out of his lips and down his beard, staining it even more crimson than it was.

His oath ... Broken. All their oaths ... turned to shit.

Oathbreakers, damned into the pit of Nidhogg, their souls to be feasted upon for eternity in the worst possible torment imaginable. Worst save perhaps for the torment of being betrayed. Of losing ... losing ...

*I give you my oath of love, Hervor.*

Lost.

One of his feet gave out beneath him and he slammed down on his knee, the pain of that barely registering next to the other agonies already consuming him. To see daylight again ...

To escape this ...

"You are bleeding rather profusely."

A woman's voice, but Starkad had not the strength to turn and look. Maybe never the strength to trust a woman again.

Arete strolled around in front of him and crouched, level with him. She dipped a long-nailed finger into his beard, pulled it back bloody, and stuck it in her mouth, sucking it like the taste alone had her in ecstasy. "Mmmmmhmmm. *Oh*, yes." She licked her lips. "Ancient, powerful ..." Her face suddenly turned down, and she pursed her lips. "And poisoned. Bleh."

Starkad glared at her. Given the choice, maybe he'd have killed her. If one oath was broken, why not all of them? How could his word mean aught anymore?

"Well," Arete said, and drew her finger along his cheek, seeming careful of his nigh-unhinged jaw. "I'd offer you immortality once more, but I guess you can't really answer, can you?" She murmured something nonsensical to herself. "No. I suppose, then, I will simply have to take silence as assent."

Starkad lurched away from her, trying to bring up the torch to swat her.

Arete caught his arm, sneered at him, and shook her head. A swift twist of her wrist sent the torch clattering out of his hand. "That was uncalled for. I'm giving you eternal life. One day, maybe, you'll be grateful for it. I will fulfill the full promise of the bargain the Ás king tempted you with. I will make you whole, and more than whole."

Another lie from another treacherous woman.

He scrambled away on his arse, making almost no progress.

The vampire woman suddenly grabbed him, one hand under his legs, the other around the back of his neck, and hefted him up. "I advise you not to scorn the gift. If your behavior continues, you will leave me no choice but to let you wither away. Either way, I think one thing has become abundantly clear, Starkad. One thing surely even you must admit now. There is no way back to the life you have known."

And all oaths were broken.

Arete had brought Starkad to a dark chamber. Maybe he was beneath Nikolaos's palace, he wasn't sure. She'd laid him upon a stone slab. This place could've been a crypt. He had not the strength to care, so he'd closed his eyes, drifting in and out of consciousness.

At one point, he realized someone had bandaged his jaw. The bandages had soaked through with blood. It wouldn't be too much longer now, and Hel would have him.

Even the pain had grown dim, distant, as Arete shook him, forcing him to look at her with his hazy eye.

"It is not easy, what I intend, and it requires you to drink the blood of Kvasir, our most sacred relic. I have procured a sip for you, Starkad." Arete frowned. "But you have to drink willingly. One way or another, you'll die soon. When that happens, your soul will be lost in the Penumbra. Or … it could be bound here, tied to your corpse that you might go on with beautiful unlife. Choose immortality … and I will prepare the ritual."

He grunted, unable to speak. To choose it … She'd

offered it to him before and he'd scorned the gift. Maybe he'd been a fool then. He'd walked away from immortality for Vikar's sake and look where that had brought him.

But then, he'd accepted Odin's foul bargain, betrayed Vikar to buy himself a few years' more life. The Ás's spell had changed him, warped him into something not quite human. But still *close* to a man. What Arete offered—there could be no deluding himself into thinking he could hold onto his humanity after this.

Then again, what had humanity given him? Blood and death and betrayal. Everyone he'd cared for was gone or had turned on him. Even Hervor. Especially Hervor.

His dark urd had brought him here.

Arete was holding a bronze goblet in one hand, the other on Starkad's chest. "Choose. Before it is too late. If you would claim what I offer, you must do so soon. I need time to prepare."

Choose ...?

As if life or urd had given him so very many choices. No, the strands of fate had guided him from one crime to the next. A strange, twisted life had brought him—a betrayer, a murderer—into the arms of one who'd visited those same crimes back upon him.

Urd.

Long had he wished to deny it, to hope he might be the master of his own existence. Hubris, perhaps. For urd bound all lives together.

Starkad had walked away from immortality and that mistake had haunted him, until he'd leapt at Odin's terrible bargain for a fraction of what he'd truly wanted. There would be no coming back if he turned from the gift a second time. No, he'd surely be bound for the gates of Hel.

Maybe he deserved that, too. But some part of him

wanted to forestall that end. To hold back the final darkness, and to ... to be revenged upon those who had brought him here, urd or no.

Ironic, really. The strange, winding cycles of vengeance had bound Hervor to Orvar-Oddr and the both of them to Starkad. An unending circle of blood. Why then should this not become the next step?

Trying to fix Arete with his one good eye, he gave a slight nod. All he could offer in his current state. Odin had brought darkness into Starkad's soul. This seemed but the extension of what the Ás king had begun so many years ago.

Arete smiled—showing her fangs—and squeezed his hand. Then she drew away and bit her arm. She smeared the blood on her fingers, knelt and began drawing something on the floor.

Starkad shut his eyes, letting out a shuddering breath. A coldness was seeping into his limbs. Hel's breath was on his face. He could almost feel the servants of the dark goddess circling, clawing their way closer to his soul. Climbing up over his legs—they prickled with gooseflesh and needles. The damned were coming for him, coming to bring home one of their own.

His heartbeat was already slowing. Too much blood loss. Not even Odin's dark spell could abate the inevitable end of such a wound as Hervor had dealt him.

He tried to flicker his eyes open, only saw shadows. Plays of light and darkness. Arete had lit candles, flitting across the room, seeming a wraith, almost.

Hard to breathe ...

The ghost was at his side, tilting his head up. Forcing his lips apart a hair, the movement further ripping his jaw. She poured something hot into his mouth and over his wound. The taste of iron, of copper. Warm at first, then icy as it settled in his gut. The only thing he still clearly felt. Even the pain was finally gone.

"I wish I could tell you not to be afraid. Everything has its price. I will incant the ritual to help bind your soul to your corpse."

Corpse?

"Before it is finished, I need to kill you."

Her voice sounded so far away. The play of light and shadow dimmed, fading slowly into blackness. Her voice changed in tone, now speaking the alien words of the Otherworlds. The sounds seemed to bombard his skull like a crushing weight. They bore down upon his chest.

Upon his face.

The pressure increased and the words grew louder. They echoed off the walls and reverberated off the air itself. A hint of vision came back to him, dim and cool, as if color and warmth had been siphoned out of the world.

And in the shadows, creatures drew nigh, crawling on all fours like lizards, though they looked somewhat like foul perversions of the human form. Hairless, with skin that bled off wisps of shadow. Eyes that gleamed with cold blue light. And teeth like fangs, a whole maw of them, like a shark's.

The creatures skittered closer to him, crawling up the stone slab where he lay immobilized, dying. With razor-sharp claws, one of them scrambled up along his legs, tearing dozens upon dozens of tiny cuts along his shins, then his thighs. Then his gut.

One of them had bitten his wrist.

Another was gnawing on one of his biceps.

A third dug a claw into his forehead and used it to begin peeling back the skin. Flaying him.

Fresh pains washed over him in waves of torment.

The words stopped and a fresh bite burned into his neck. His blood seeped out, leaving him cold.

Everything went hazy, faded into nigh total blackness for a heartbeat. His *last* heartbeat. His lungs exploded and the pressure was gone. His vision snapped back, revealing the hideous creatures gorging themselves upon his flesh. And he could move.

Starkad bucked, trying to dislodge the abominations. He managed only to topple from the slab and land in a great heap along with three of these things. They clawed and bit and tore at him.

Arete's words once more rang out, a cacophony in this shadowy world, demanding and unrelenting, even if Starkad could not understand them. He roared, twisted around, and managed to pin one of the things underneath him. He slammed a fist into its skull.

Then he jerked his elbow back into the maw of another. That sent it toppling over backward, leaving just the one gnawing on his thigh. With a great cry, he slammed his palms together on both sides of its temples.

As expected, the creature collapsed, clutching its head and rolling over onto its back.

Starkad tried to stand, but his legs gave out. His heart wasn't beating, but still, something coursed through his veins. Warm. Powerful.

His hands were shaking.

Arete was still beside the altar, now a mere shadow, a trick of the light, her movements slow, as if through quicksand. As Starkad watched, though, her form flickered. It seemed to split in half, a ghostly apparition ripping itself partway out of her. Her double was etheric and yet more clearly real and distinct than her other form had been.

And it was looking at him, reaching a hand out toward

him. "The blood of Kvasir holds you bound. Come back to us ..."

Her words bent, distorted as if underwater. His head felt full of wool, thick and wobbly.

But she was there, hand waiting for him to take it.

Starkad lunged forward and wrapped his hand around her wrist. Hers closed on his. Solid as aught.

And she jerked him up, off the ground and toward her. She wrapped her arms around him, kissed him, blood dribbling over his lips. Her blood or his, he couldn't say.

An uncontrolled shudder built in his gut and spread out until his entire body was convulsing, held in place only by her arms.

Blinding white light flashed in front of his eyes, then darkness.

## 25

*B*lessed daylight had already cracked through the sky when Hervor climbed the ladder, pushed aside the grate, and managed to crawl up into an alley. She surely reeked of shit and sweat and Odin knew what else. Hardly seemed to matter. Grunting with exhaustion, she crawled over to the side of a building and huddled down against it, squinting in the sunlight.

Fuck ... Starkad ... he was dead. She murdered her lover. She pressed her palms into her eyes. Hel take Orvar-Oddr. He'd ... finally done it. He'd destroyed everything she cared for. He'd fucking taken it all!

She choked on the lump in her throat, struggled to swallow, then coughed. Breathing seemed nigh to impossible. Hel ... Why hadn't he just killed her? He should've killed her.

Maybe he still would. If she just laid here, sooner or later he'd track her down. Would he come out into the light of day? Maybe. He'd done it before. Even without his Otherworldly powers, Orvar could still best her, especially in her current state and her having naught but a knife to defend herself with.

Why had she done it? Why?

Odin's stones, maybe she ought to just wait here and let Orvar end her. She was so godsdamned tired of ... everything. All of it was troll shit.

And still, *still* she couldn't sit here and wait to die.

Teeth grit against the pain and fatigue and sheer brain-searing despondency, she forced herself up, stumbled out into the market, and then glared at the passersby who made faces at her stench. They could all rot behind the gates of Hel and she'd care naught.

Why fight the inevitable end? She had naught left to live for, did she?

She pushed her way through the crowd—most gave her a wide berth before she reached them anyway—heading in a random direction. She hardly much cared where she ended up, so long as it was away from the Arrow's Point. And Tanna. And fucking Nikolaos.

Everything was troll shit.

But she just wasn't the giving up type. She'd lived well enough before meeting Starkad Eightarms.

Except she couldn't quite remember what that felt like anymore. Couldn't remember that life as more than a dream. And now she was in a nightmare. Orvar-Oddr had haunted her for so long. Finally got his vengeance. So maybe now he'd be looking to end her.

Hervor stumbled into another alley, found some empty barrels, and collapsed down behind them. She needed to rest. To think. To figure out where to go from here. She just ...

The fucking draug had taken everything from her. The

last thing, the least ... she could do, would be to put him out of his godsdamned misery. That was it, then.

She was going to kill the Arrow's Point one more time.

Or die trying.

Either way, this had to end.

&.

THE HAND on her shoulder jolted Hervor awake and she reached for a knife. An iron grip caught her wrist and held it still. She thrashed a moment before she recognized Vebiorg, crouched over her. Behind the varulf, Win was standing, glancing this way and that down the alley.

The sun had dipped low. How long had she slept? Her stomach growled as Vebiorg helped her up.

"What do you want?" Hervor asked.

The varulf shrugged. "We thought you'd want to know. The vampire bitch took Starkad. Mentioned ... changing him."

"He's alive?" That was ... impossible. No human could survive Tyrfing's poison. But Vebiorg seemed every bit in earnest.

"Not for long." Win said from the alley entrance. "If the vampire has her way, he'll be one of them. Maybe already is, I don't know. All I could do was get the sword and get out of there. If Vebiorg hadn't found me, I'd probably still be wandering in the damned tunnels."

The sword ... He had Tyrfing slung over his shoulder.

Hervor glared at the hateful thing. Even looking at it made her heart long to hold it once more. Seeing it hanging over another's shoulder was an icy spear through her gut. Reason enough to cut his bowels out. Or run far from here.

What had her father said in his barrow, so long ago?

She'd ignored his warnings about the sword's curse. He'd said it would bring her woe, but she'd taken no heed. Probably Angantyr could not have even imagined how true his warning would prove.

She climbed to her feet. "Give me the runeblade. It is my family's legacy." Their curse.

"Ah," Win said. "Is it now? A legacy stolen from my father's predecessor, entrusted by Gylfi to protect Holmgard."

"I'm not certain that sword protects aught. Either way, though, it is bound to me and I *will* have it. I'm going to kill Orvar-Oddr with it once more and put an end to this."

Win unshouldered the blade, holding it by the sheath. "And if I refuse? Suppose I decide to carry this back to my kingdom and return it to the task it was meant for?"

Hervor shook her head and snickered. "Meant for? It was crafted by the dvergar as a means to earn favor with the Old Kingdoms while subverting them at the same time. The runeblades are cursed, Win, all of them. Trust me when I say you do not want it."

The prince looked at the sheathed sword. "I am not certain you deserve any measure of trust, shieldmaiden. But our mission here remains unchanged and Vebiorg convinced me that, whatever crimes lay in your past, with Eightarms taken, you may prove our best chance at victory."

Victory against Tanna seemed a fool's dream at this point. She'd settle for avenging herself on Orvar-Oddr. If she lived through that, maybe she'd just leave Miklagard. Her oaths to Starkad were already broken. Next to that, her oaths to Rollaugr meant very little. She reached out a hand for the blade, and Win finally handed it over.

"What of Starkad?" Vebiorg asked.

Funny, it always came back to that question for Hervor.

For Starkad she'd gone to Glaesisvellir. For Starkad, she'd chanced the wastes of Pohjola. And for Starkad she had come here, thinking to find human foes, and instead encountering monsters more terrible than aught she had ever faced.

Her oath was broken ... but still it bound her. "I cannot abandon him while there is yet breath left in his body."

Vebiorg growled. "If the vampire bitch succeeds, maybe he won't have breath left at all."

"Then we have to reach him before that happens. We know where Nikolaos's palace lies."

Win glanced out into the alley. "The sun is already setting. The vampires will be at full strength now."

Hervor nodded. "Maybe, but we cannot delay any longer." Not if they were to have any chance of recovering Starkad.

"These creatures were our only allies in the city," Win said. "If we turn on them ..."

Hervor shook her head. "If they are allies, they will not bar our reunion with Starkad." She did not need to say what would happen if they were enemies.

## 26

The sudden return of awareness struck him like a bolt of lightning. Starkad lurched upward, drew a reflexive breath that he didn't feel fill up his lungs, and looked around. He sat upon the same stone slab Arete had brought him to.

Runes were painted in blood in a circle around the stone, with a ring of candles beyond those. Arete herself lay on another slab, her eyes closed.

The pain in his jaw had faded to a dull ache, though his mouth felt bloated. As his tongue brushed over his teeth, he knew why. His upper canines had grown sharp as spear points, and a hint elongated maybe. He grunted, unable to make sense of the strange flurry of sensations flooding over his senses.

Countless aches remained from all the injuries he'd suffered, but none of them bothered him overmuch. His whole body trembled, though, feeling weak. His vision was still a bit hazy. And ... He shut his right eye and all went dark.

Damn it.

He'd dared to hope whatever Arete had done to him might restore his vision, but his left eye was still dead and his right remained clouded over.

When he opened his eye again, Arete had sat up and strode to the door. She shouted something in Miklagardian outside, then shut the door and came to Starkad's side.

"I know you have questions. Night has fallen and that is our time. Before aught else, you must feed and regain your strength. I took every last drop of your blood. A necessary part of the spell, I'm afraid."

He tried to rise, but his legs gave out, and Arete caught him in her arms.

"Shhh. Just wait."

Out in the hall, he could hear the sound of a heart beating. Growing closer.

He tried to lunge toward the noise, not even sure why he was doing it, but Arete held him in place, her arms iron bands.

A moment later, the door opened and a hand shoved a girl into the room. She stumbled, fell to her knees, and looked up at him through a tangle of hair covering her face. She wore naught but a thin robe, and her hands were chained behind her back. A slave. A prisoner.

"There now," Arete said. "Eat her."

Eat ... a person ... The thought buzzed in his head, awful and inescapable, demanding his utmost devotion. It thrummed through his chest. He knelt beside her, not even sure how he'd gotten there or when he'd left Arete's arms. But his hands were snared up in the girl's robe. With a savage jerk he tore it open, exposing her pale breasts.

Like Hervor's, albeit without the scar she now bore.

Starkad lunged forward, bore the girl to the ground and bit into one of her breasts. She shrieked, but he barely heard her. Hot blood streamed down his throat, sweeter than mead and more sating than venison. Except that he needed more and more. He tore himself free of her breast—her thrashing had already become faint—and then sank his fangs into her neck, sucking so hard his throat hurt.

Slurping noisily, devouring her whole. Her blood, her life force seeped into him, like tasting her very soul. Beautiful and lonely and frightened, all drawn deep inside him, replenishing him. Warmth spread into his limbs, his fingertips. His toes. A pulse pounded through him, though he knew his heart did not beat.

"He's going to need another," Arete said behind him.

Starkad didn't look at her, couldn't tear himself away from the girl. Her breath had almost given out. Her hopes, dreams, fears ... all slipping away. The blood he drew from her had become a trickle when he craved a fountain of it.

And as if in answer, more heartbeats sounded out in the hall.

Another vampire—no heartbeat—flung a second girl into the room, then shut the door once more. Starkad dropped the first, then launched himself onto the next. He grasped her neck, hesitated. Her smell was luxurious. Sweet and heady. Uncertain even what he meant to do, he pulled her robe up past her hips. She wore naught below them.

A feral urge seized him and he leaned low, licked his tongue over the girl's trench. She shuddered, moaned. Before he knew he'd planned it, he sunk his teeth into her thigh. Her moan turned into a gasp of pain, a whimper. Starkad grabbed her hips and hefted her up so he could rise into a sitting position.

He drank and drank, until her whimpers grew faint.

"Are you not sated? I can give you what else you crave ..."

Starkad dropped the girl and she lay on the stone floor, shivering. Ignoring her, he spun toward Arete.

The vampire leaned against the stone slab, staring at him with mischievous eyes and a faint smile. "The blood pounding now, coursing to *every* part of your body. Alive with fresh sensations and craving every pleasure of the flesh. You cannot eat, save for blood, but you can yet enjoy other temptations denied to many of the dead. We are blessed by the gift of—"

Starkad lunged at her, seeming almost to fly off the ground, and tackled her back onto the slab. Arete chuckled as Starkad ripped her golden dress down the middle. He lathered his tongue over her breasts and she drew her nails down along his back. From the warmth that dribbled down there, she must've drawn blood.

He didn't fucking care.

Wished he could hold it back, draw this out. But he couldn't stand it. He tore the rest of her dress until he got to the bush of black hair between her legs. She snapped the ties to his trousers with ease and yanked them down, as if he'd need the help or encouragement. He buried himself inside her, pumping away with more fervor and power than he'd ever felt.

Grinding, until the stone creaked beneath her. Until they were both screaming in release.

Then she traced a lazy hand along the back of his neck. "Finish your meal, then we can do this again. It's always best just after feeding. Things grow cold if you go too long without fresh blood, then everything ceases to function as you might wish."

He turned, looked at the wretched, half-naked girl trying to crawl to the door. He'd already murdered one person today. He wouldn't take another life. Not another ...

Except he was already on top of her, fangs piercing her throat.

o Hervor's great surprise, Nikolaos's slaves admitted her and the others to the palace and even agreed to escort them to where Starkad was resting. While not having to fight them was a relief, their reaction did not bode well. Her gut roiled at the thought of why they would not bar her from seeing Starkad. Especially given what Win claimed to have overheard Arete say.

And Hervor could think of but one reason they would not stop her.

Because it was too late.

And Starkad was …

No. No, she would not allow herself to think that. No.

Because if Arete had slain him and turned him into some kind of deathless abomination like the other vampires … it would be Hervor's fault. Hers was the blade that had mortally wounded Starkad. Hers were the crimes and lies that had led to that fight in the first place. And much as she wanted to lay all the blame at the feet of the Arrow's Point, her churning stomach would not allow that much self-delusion.

"Calm yourself," Vebiorg whispered by her side.

"I am ..." It was hard to swallow. Hard to even make the words come out. "I am left with the awful realization that maybe a life of blood and murder can only end one way. The same way it was lived."

Vebiorg snorted. "A child ought to know as much. Have you so deluded yourself to believe that there is no price to be paid for the things we do?" The varulf shook her head. "There is only one way a bad life ends—badly."

Hervor clenched her jaw and said naught. How could she argue with such words?

Win grabbed her wrist. "Keep your head clear. There is a time and place for macabre rumination, but never while in peril. If it comforts you, consider: a violent life is like to end in violence. But a great many peaceful lives end in violence, too. Such is the weave of urd and the will of the Aesir. We have but our parts to play in a greater tapestry."

She tried to take comfort in Win's words, but his fatalism seemed a bitter draught at best.

The slave led them down some stairs and through darkened halls. The rooms lining the halls might well have been cells to hold prisoners for all she knew. But if they held Starkad prisoner, why freely walk her and the others down here? Did they lay an ambush at the end of this path?

At a bend, the slave paused and inclined his head, speaking in broken Northern. "Please use left door."

Hervor didn't bother to further acknowledge the man, just hurried down the hall. The sound of grunting reached her before she got to the room. Was he hurt? Still dying from his wound? Or was the bitch trying to turn him even now?

Breaking into a trot, Hervor raced to the door, flung it open, and darted inside.

Starkad and Arete were there, both naked, and he had her shoved up against the wall, pounding into her trench with impressive fervor.

Starkad cast a glance her way, bared his teeth. Fangs. And kept right on fucking Arete. She squealed, laughed, her legs locked behind Starkad's back. The bitch moaned louder than necessary, clearly for Hervor's benefit.

Hervor backed up, hit the doorframe, and fumbled, unsure whether her hand was reaching to cover her mouth or go for her sword.

Beside her, Win groaned in disgust and fled the room, while Vebiorg stared with apparent interest.

"Starkad ..." Hervor whimpered. "Starkad ..."

Odin's ... why wasn't he stopping? He just kept pumping into the vampire, on and on.

That roil in Hervor's stomach had grown to an icy hand, squeezing her heart and taking her breath away. Choking her. Killing her with its slow, inevitable pressure.

"You made oathbreakers of us both," Starkad said, not looking at her.

Strange he wasn't even out of breath. Stranger, she had trouble wrapping her mind around his words. They were there. She'd heard them. But it just didn't seem clear.

He was saying ... saying ...

He just kept staring at Arete's face.

Vebiorg grabbed Hervor's arm and pulled her away, out of the hall and after Win who stood waiting for them by the slave, studiously staring at his feet.

They knew. They knew what Starkad was saying. Win hadn't even heard it, and he'd known.

He wasn't the fool Hervor was.

Anyone could see it. Starkad was saying he was done

with Hervor. That she wasn't even worthy of the effort of killing for her mistakes.

That she was worthy of naught at all.

❦

"YOUR PACK all died when you were young," Hervor said to Vebiorg, her voice sounding dry in her ears. "If you knew who killed them, you'd have avenged them, yes?"

The varulf woman nodded, walking alongside Hervor while casting furtive glances to either side as they stalked the alleys. "Of course."

Win had taken charge and insisted they needed to make it off the streets. Going back to the apartment was too great a risk, considering Afrid knew of it. They could not wander the streets at night any longer than they must, though, so the prince was hunting for any place they could take shelter.

Accord to Win, Hervor seemed in no shape to finish the mission and slay Tanna. So they'd retreat, rest until sunrise, and then break into his palace and rescue Höfund. Somehow, the prince still believed they'd kill the Patriarch and steal Mistilteinn. And then escape to the harbor.

All Hervor wanted now was to kill the Arrow's Point. But she'd fight alongside Vebiorg and Win. She'd fight with them, maybe die with them. Really, they were all she had left. And maybe her best chance to overcome either vampires or a draug.

"Why ask such a thing?" the varulf asked a moment later.

Oh. Vengeance. Beautiful. Horrible. Dark. Bloody.

Hervor couldn't even swallow. "Orvar-Oddr helped murder my father and all his brothers. And I found that out and I came after him. And I infiltrated his crew, bided my time, and killed him when the opportunity presented itself."

Vebiorg grunted. "So you murdered him instead of challenging him to a holmgang and doing it the right way."

"I couldn't have won that way."

"Then you didn't deserve to kill him, did you?"

Hervor flinched. "Wolves don't catch their foes out by surprise?"

The varulf shrugged. "I'm not the one looking for justification for my crimes."

"I don't have to justify myself to anyone!"

"Then stop trying. Your mistake cost you and it cost all of us." Vebiorg sniffed. "Then again, we've all made our share of mistakes." She shrugged. "It's life."

"This one," Win said, pointing to a soaring building where the dome had cracked and a great chunk of it had fallen inside. The tip remained, probably forty feet in the air, while the surrounding structure covered at least a hundred feet on the long sides. Maybe it had once been a temple of some kind, but Hervor knew less than naught about Miklagardian religion, assuming the locals even had one.

To reach the structure, they'd have to cross a wide open street, though. A faint mist drifted over a cobblestone road maybe twenty feet across. They could dash from the alley, reach the intersection to the main street, and be close to the building in the space of a few heartbeats. But those heartbeats would be time they spent exposed to anyone watching.

Still, part of the wall had cracked, too, exposing a window maybe eight feet up. One big enough for them to fit through and drop inside, finding shelter from the night. Their best chance, probably.

Rest a little, wait for daylight.

Just make it across the street first.

"Ready?" Win asked.

Vebiorg sniffed, glanced both ways, and took off at a dash Hervor would have been hard-pressed to match on a godsdamned horse. She raced after the varulf, but the other woman had leapt up and caught the windowsill before Hervor was even into the temple's yard.

She and Win reached the building, panting, and Vebiorg extended a hand down to them, one of her legs resting inside the building, one out. Hervor took her hand and the varulf jerked her up to the sill beside her. Then Hervor dropped down inside.

In here, the architecture seemed even more imposing than the outside had. Great marble columns supported a roof, several of these cracked where sections of that roof had collapsed into piles of rubble blocking a central walkway to the back of the temple. The dome lay over a circular mosaic in the floor, but the fallen pieces from above had shattered whatever design had once lain below. Some of those stones now littering the floor were bigger than Hervor was.

She couldn't imagine what it took to build something like this. A place maybe even beyond the knowledge of the Old Kingdoms. It almost seemed as if gods themselves had raised up the temple in some age long past. How and why the Miklagardians had allowed it to fall into such disrepair, she had no idea.

Win and Vebiorg had also dropped down to the ground, and the two of them slunk to the back of the temple, into a semi-circular alcove where the floor was slightly raised. They both lay down there, clearly as tired as Hervor felt.

They had the right of it. And part of Hervor wanted to lay down right beside them.

Wanted to hold on to them and believe she could call

them friends. But how could they trust her, knowing what they knew? No, they tolerated her because they needed her. Naught else.

So best to keep her distance, give them space.

After strolling the temple a bit, Hervor slumped down by the mosaic. Through the hole in the roof, she could see the stars.

SHE DIDN'T SLEEP. For a long time she watched the night sky. Then she watched the others as they slept. She stared at Tyrfing's golden hilt. Maybe she should have heeded her father's ghost and left it buried in the barrow.

Maybe she should have done a great many things different.

Rather pointless to muse on that now, though.

All that remained now was to finish what she'd started. The skalds would've liked that.

She'd started out to kill the Arrow's Point, and now she'd be doing the same—

A shadow blocked out the moonlight and Hervor looked up to see a man dropping down from the dome above. She scooted a foot away an instant before Orvar-Oddr crashed down in the middle of the mosaic. His impact further crunched the stones, sending dust and debris flying as he landed in a crouch, then lifted his red, gleaming eyes to her. Snarling, teeth bared.

Hervor scrambled away, jerked Tyrfing free, and just managed to get her own feet as Orvar rose. Behind him, Vebiorg and Win had leapt up as well.

Orvar chuckled, the sound an assault on Hervor's brain. The hideous, tormented mirth of the damned. "And now the last one you care for is dead. By your own hand no less. I could not have wrought my vengeance more perfectly. Only one thing yet remains. I will feast upon your black, withered heart and send what remains of your soul screaming down to Hel. Then your torture shall truly begin." The draug pulled a broadsword from over his shoulder and spun as Win and Vebiorg raced forward.

The varulf reached him first, already changed into a wolf. The draug twisted out of the way of her lunge and the wolf flew by him. Unwilling to give up the edge that granted, Hervor darted in, swinging Tyrfing in a tight arc.

Orvar parried that, turned, knocked aside Win's thrusting sword, and then danced back around to keep them both ahead of him. He was fast. Faster than a man now, it seemed. Maybe not as fast as both her and Win at the same time, though.

She glanced at the prince, he nodded, and together they charged in.

Vebiorg snarled, perhaps blocked from her attack angle. Hervor couldn't well look at her. She swung high as Win went low. Orvar parried Tyrfing, let Win's broadsword cleave into his thigh, and twisted around behind the prince. He caught Win's arm, spun him between himself and Hervor, turning the prince around backward in one move. Then he thrust his sword up through Win's armpit.

A sickening scrape of metal over bone and then Orvar jerked the blade free and flung Win's corpse at Hervor. She tried to step out of the way but Win's arms tangled in hers and she fell to the ground.

Vebiorg leapt over the pair of them, snapping and snarling in unconcealed rage.

Hervor shoved Win's corpse off herself, scrambled to her feet, and came about to see Vebiorg rip a chunk of putrefying flesh out of Orvar's calf. The wound ought to have dropped him. Strands of muscle and sinew were hanging loose, dragging on the floor behind him. He was shrieking in pain, the sound even more mind-rending than his laughter. Made Hervor want to clutch her ears and duck and pray to the Aesir for safety from the damned.

But Odin wasn't here and, so far as Hervor could tell, hadn't done troll shit about Orvar-Oddr thus far. The Ás didn't seem like to start now.

Bellowing her own war cry that only half drowned out the hideous shrieking in her skull, Hervor charged in, swiping again and again. Tyrfing managed to sneak past Orvar's defenses and rend the mail on his arm, but even that only stoked the draug's fury.

He caught her next blow on his broadsword, slid the blade up until he was matching strength with her. Which was no contest, but she couldn't let go or he'd drive his blade through her face. Instead, he shoved her backward, actually lifting her off her feet.

Hervor managed to land on one knee, sucking in her breath at the pain from knocking her other one on the stone floor.

Vebiorg lunged in, flying for his throat. The draug's backhand caught her across the muzzle and sent her careening to the floor.

Hervor rose, panting.

Orvar bent over and snared up a rock the size of Hervor's torso.

Oh, Odin's lumpy stones.

The draug flung the stone and Hervor dove to the floor. The projectile swooshed over her head, ruffling her hair in its passage. She launched herself upward, swinging Tyrfing as she did so, following an arc that ought to have cut his cock off and split him up to his neck.

The draug flung himself forward before her arc got full momentum, slammed into her chest, and knocked the wind from her. Tyrfing toppled from her grasp as a haze of white filled her vision. She hit the ground hard. Couldn't see. Couldn't hear.

Couldn't breathe.

She gasped, trying to fill her lungs.

"... is fitting, don't you think?" What the fuck was the draug saying now? His hollow, grating voice tore at her mind.

Hervor managed to lift her head off the rock. The bastard was holding Tyrfing himself now, pale blue flames dancing along the blade. "Your father died wielding this against Hjalmar, though he killed his foe as well. I rather think this blade wounded them both. And now it will kill his daughter, who could not let the past lay buried."

With another snarl, Vebiorg flew at him and her jaw closed down on his left forearm, the one holding Tyrfing. The blade clattered from his hand as well. She must've had nigh to his strength, because she yanked him to the ground as well.

Hervor lunged at Tyrfing, caught its hilt, and then thrust at Orvar-Oddr. The draug whipped the wolf around and Hervor barely managed to pull her attack short and avoid impaling the varulf. Instead, Vebiorg slammed into Hervor and sent the both of them toppling over.

Limping and lilting from side to side, Orvar tromped over, caught Vebiorg by the scruff of her neck, and flung her two dozen feet. The varulf collided with a column in mid-air, cracked it, and crashed hard into the floor.

Orvar growled at Hervor, dark liquid dribbling down his chin. "Just you and I, as it should be."

Hervor managed her feet, holding Tyrfing up between her and the draug. "I will end you. Whatever it fucking takes. I'm going to cut you down. You took ... *everything* from me!"

The draug just bared his teeth once more, visage dark and Otherworldly.

Hervor didn't give a fuck anymore. She was tired of being scared. Shrieking, Tyrfing grasped in both hands, she charged in. The pale flames along the blade flared higher, mirroring her rage.

She cleaved straight down onto Orvar. He twisted out of the way of that, so Hervor feinted left, reversed her swing, and cut back at him. The runeblade bit deep into his gut and the draug stumbled back, snarling.

Not letting up, Hervor lunged in again. Her arms burned with fatigue, muscles flimsy as water. She let fury make up for her failing strength, slicing back and forth, an endless stream of attacks.

Orvar parried, dodged, knocked her blade aside. She just kept coming on, snarling like the mindless horror he had become. Tyrfing flashed up and ripped through his left elbow, leaving his forearm dangling by strands of rotting flesh.

Almost the same instant, his sword slammed into her abdomen. Her mail kept it from cleaving her in half. Barely. The blow heaved her off her feet. Dug mail links into her flesh even through her leather pads. Sent vomit spewing out of her even as she flew backward and crashed down to the floor.

Insides crushed ... couldn't ... move.

Hervor gasped, gurgled on vomit. Struggled to suck down a breath.

Another snarl, and Vebiorg flew into Orvar once more. The draug's sword flew free as the varulf barreled him over. They were on the floor too, Orvar struggling to hold the wolf back from his throat with one remaining arm. Had his forearm against her neck, pressing her back, barely keeping snapping fangs from tearing out his face.

Fuck.

Hervor had to get over there. Had to help Vebiorg before the draug could recover.

Groaning, she managed to roll over to her side. Started to crawl for Tyrfing. Please, Odin. Give her just a little more strength. Moments more to end this. Just one more chance …

Vebiorg yelped, snarled in pain.

Grunting, Hervor cast a look over her shoulder. The varulf had arched her back, twitching as her form shifted. Audible pops as bones changed shape, the woman thrashing in obvious pain.

Sunlight just peeking through the hole in the roof.

Oh, Odin's stones. Vebiorg …

Frantic, Hervor crawled faster, pulled herself to Tyrfing. Closed her hand around its hilt. The pain in her gut dimmed ever so slightly as the runeblade's rage seeped into her. Rapid breaths, trying to steady herself, pull herself to her knees.

Vebiorg was naked, resting on hands and knees in the circle of sunlight. Snarling, Orvar stalked around its perimeter. The draug couldn't get to the varulf without moving into the light and losing all his powers.

Hervor's gut dropped when she realized he wasn't

circling Vebiorg, he was moving around the light's perimeter, toward Hervor.

"Run!" Vebiorg shouted at her.

Oh, godsdamn it! Not like this. Hervor stumbled to her feet, blundered toward the rotting double doors that closed in the temple.

A hideous growl behind her as Orvar surged forward, stride uneven given his rent leg, but still faster than her. Odin's stones!

She had to move. Had to ... faster!

She reached the doors. Could feel him a few feet behind. Hervor swiped Tyrfing, the runeblade tearing through the rotting wood like it was barely there. She flung her weight at the door and crashed through, heedless of dozens of splinters piercing her arms, her legs, her face.

Beyond, she hit stone steps, toppled down them, banging her head, her shoulders, her hips. Impact after impact jarred her before she pitched down into the cobblestone street.

Gasping at the innumerable aches, she rolled over. No one out on the streets yet. Not so close to dawn. People here waited, maybe not even sure why they feared the night so very much, but sure something was out in it.

Through the ruptured door, a pair of red eyes gleamed inside the darkened temple. A roar erupted from there, vile, a shriek of defiant rage torn straight from the gates of Hel.

Teeth grit, Hervor rose, Tyrfing wobbly in her hands but raised before her.

The hatred wafting off Orvar-Oddr was almost enough to choke her, even from twenty feet away.

But he wasn't following.

Grunting in too many agonies to keep track of, Hervor

stumbled down the street, casting repeated glances at those red eyes.

They watched her every step.

§⦾

BY THE TIME she drew nigh to the harbor, the streets were thick with people, many staring at her as she limped and plodded her way past them. The rise of people had left her with no choice but to sheath Tyrfing.

Besides, she was fair certain Orvar-Oddr would not pursue her in daylight, much less in public. A draug would send most people screaming in terror, but *someone* would surely come to destroy the creature if he proved so bold. Hel, if Hervor could speak the language, she'd be half-tempted to find a Miklagardian soldier and report the draug in that temple.

No, that was pointless musing. She didn't speak the language, didn't know the name of the place, and Orvar was like to have found some shadow to crawl into, anyway.

But ... Hervor faltered. Vebiorg.

Damn it. She had to pray the varulf would make it out on her own. As far as she knew, varulfur still maintained some of their strength even in daylight. Shit, maybe Vebiorg could even kill Orvar-Oddr.

Either way, Hervor had given every last drop of rage, skill, and effort she could manage. And she'd still failed. The Arrow's Point had bested her, even with Win and Vebiorg beside her. The draug was unstoppable.

Hervor had to get the fuck out of Miklagard.

At the city gate, she had to hold up, as the guards slowly waved people through in small groups. People coming in from the harbor, those going out. All got a cursory inspection. Maybe they'd stop her considering her obvious wounds. Maybe not.

Either way, the throng gathered there meant waiting around for her chance. She had plenty of silver plundered from Tanna's vault. She could use that to take a boat. At this point, it mattered little where it was bound. Miklagard seemed perched on the edge of the gates of Hel, so most anywhere would be an improvement.

Pausing, even for the brief moment, only made the pains worse. More obvious. She ought to be lying abed for a fortnight. If there was a ship bound for Bjarmaland, could she even make the trek back to Holmgard?

She leaned on a building wedged against the city wall. Barely stifled her groans and pants, and that only because she didn't want the crowd staring at her. If she fled to Bjarmaland, Orvar-Oddr would follow. His hatred was as undying as his body. He'd stolen Starkad from her—the man fucking that vampire bitch made that clear enough.

The draug would hunt her every last day of her life, however long or short that proved. She was so godsdamned tired of being afraid. Of looking for red eyes in every shadow. Of waiting to see who would be found dead next. She drew in a sharp breath.

*There is only one way a bad life ends—badly.*

Vebiorg was right on that count. Hervor had wrought her own urd. Lived as a bandit, a pirate. A murderer. Committed nigh every crime imaginable. Except, she'd never broken an oath until now.

She'd sworn vengeance on Orvar-Oddr, and she'd taken it. Maybe that had been a mistake, but she'd kept her oath.

People began to step around her, thinking she no longer waited for the chance to pass the gate. Maybe she no longer did. Because she still had an oath to Starkad. Maybe she could make him see her side of it.

Maybe not.

But she had to try.

And she had to go after Orvar. Become the hunter.

One way or another, she had to put an end to this.

## 28

*A*rete had seen to Starkad's needs, predicted them all. Through the haze of his death and rebirth, it had proved nigh impossible to control himself or make sense of the flood of sensations. In the aftermath, though, he'd looked upon the carnage he'd wrought.

It was the distant horror of a battlefield. The stench of death and the disquiet of knowing he'd had a hand in it, yet it remained far away. Removed from him, as if it had been someone else's hand that dealt the killing blows.

Now he stood in front of Tanna's palace, staring up at the massive wall around it. Maybe the Patriarch would be in his tower.

That thought had run round and round in Starkad's head and given him pause, while forcing him to dwell on the events of his first waking two nights ago.

The heartbreak on Hervor's face had offered a dim satisfaction. The pain she visited upon him returned to her in some small portion. All of it seemed a blur, though.

With the victims and the fucking both, he felt like he had wandered back into the nightmare worlds Ogn had drawn him through. Except this was reality, he was fair certain. And he had become something like a draug now, creatures he had despised and seen as foes most of his life. Creatures that killed many he'd known and cared for. Abominations.

As a vampire, was he better than a draug for being less obsessed with vengeance, perhaps even closer to human? Or was he worse, for those very same reasons? Because he was not driven by the single-minded pursuit of destroying the living and yet found himself preying upon them all the same.

Hard to say, really.

At the moment, though, he did not seek to prey upon humans but upon other vampires. A bold ambition, perhaps.

Arete had warned him he was young, barely in control of himself. The latter had probably been true most of his life. She'd said Tanna had vampires serving him who'd lived for centuries, stoking their power by devouring countless victims' life energies. Starkad could not hope to match that, she'd said.

Then again, he'd fought Tanna and lived, even as a mortal. And he was something more than that now.

Starkad grasped the gate and heaved himself upward, caught the top of it, and slipped over. His increased strength made most barriers mere minor annoyances. Useful.

Beyond the wall, a heartbeat pounded. Just one. Poor bastard.

Starkad crept forward, sticking to the shadows. A single guard patrolled around the yard, though other heartbeats sounded in the distance. They should have patrolled in pairs, the fools.

With incredible speed, Starkad lunged at him, slapped a

hand over his mouth, and bit down on his neck. The guard squirmed a moment before his strength—meager though it seemed next to Starkad's—gave out. Starkad drank deep, but still felt full from last night and couldn't stomach much more. Instead, he broke the man's neck and left the corpse lying there.

Whatever Arete had done, it had mostly fixed Starkad's jaw. She'd said a few more feedings and he'd be able to speak without pain. He'd complained about his eyes and she'd said those injuries were too old to be fixed by his rebirth. Meaning he was stuck with bad vision for all eternity. Delirious as he was while dying, he hadn't really considered that, and he found himself a little vexed at Arete for not bothering to point it out.

He jumped up to a windowsill ten feet in the air, pulled himself up, and slipped inside. Just beyond here, two more guards waited on a landing. He dispatched these two and pushed on.

On the upper level, he checked several rooms before coming to one with another guard. Starkad charged him from the shadows and slammed a fist into his gut before he could raise a cry. Then he snapped this one's neck too.

Starkad tried the door. Locked. He slammed against the door twice before the lock buckled. It opened into a plush bedchamber. Probably Tanna's room, though empty now. He stroked his beard, found that sent a small twinge of pain to his jaw—feeding hurt too, but it was so powerful he almost didn't notice—and gave it over.

He made his way further down the winding stairs to the lower level. Nikolaos had still refused to act directly against Tanna or even allow Arete to do so. Starkad got the impression that, as a vampire given life by Arete, the rules should have prevented him from trying this, too.

He'd made it clear he didn't give a fuck about vampire rules or the emperor or aught else save killing Tanna. And Nikolaos had ordered Arete to give Starkad two new swords, these made of pure iron. Not woven, not worked into steel, pure iron.

"We're ghosts," Arete had explained. "Pure iron—cold iron, that is—is harmful to us. The hilts are wrapped in leather, allowing you to hold them. The blades will sap your strength, though, so take care."

Some völvur had claimed iron warded against vaettir. If it worked against vampires, that was all the better.

As he reached the lower floor, a shadow dropped down from the ceiling. Starkad lurched away just as a female vampire slashed at him with claw-like nails. Shit. He'd gotten used to listening for heartbeats and hadn't noticed her. He fell back, hit the stairs, and had nowhere to go.

Nor any room to draw his blades.

Instead, he caught her wrist as she slashed at him. She jerked free with astounding strength, her other hand slashing along his face and neck. The pain of it stunned him for a bare instant, then he ducked the next blow. So she was stronger than him. Not faster, though. He dodged, hit her in the ribs with a hook, and followed up with an uppercut to her jaw. That one sent her toppling over backward.

He jerked his blades free. She leapt up, lunged at him, then drew up short as she caught sight of his swords. Too late. He rammed one through her chest. She spasmed, then went limp around it. With the other, he lopped her head off.

That ought to kill a vampire.

Starkad kicked her corpse off his blade, then started down a hall.

More heartbeats. Giving over stealth, he charged right at them, cutting both down before they even had weapons up.

Guards probably meant he was going the right way. He tore through more hapless victims and another vampire who clearly didn't expect intruders at all, much less one as fast as him. If Starkad didn't find Tanna, maybe he'd just kill every last bastard who worked for him. That ought to get the Patriarch's attention.

Starkad came to stairs leading deeper, followed them down into what seemed like a dungeon. A few prisoners in the cells, though no one Starkad recognized. He bypassed those, then paused at a cell. Beyond a steel door, chained to the wall, rested Höfund. Bruises covered the big man over more or less every spot of skin Starkad could see. That, and at least three distinct pairs of bite marks. The vampires had fed off him. And his feet were bare, both those and his shins charred black and oozing blood.

Eyelids drooping, Höfund lifted his gaze to Starkad. Actually, one of those lids didn't quite open given the heavy swelling around it. The other eye blinked, like it didn't quite believe it was him.

Starkad sheathed his swords, strode over and grasped the chains, then yanked them out of the wall. A link snapped, and Höfund pitched forward onto his hands, groaning.

"Someone turned you."

Starkad spun at the voice, hands going to the hilts of his swords.

Tanna stood there, Mistilteinn in hand, a slight smirk on his face. "I admit, I didn't think Nikolaos would go so far. Do you think he'll grieve the loss of his progeny?" Tanna hefted the runeblade. "More importantly, did you know this runeblade can kill even an immortal? The other runeblades were graced with strange gifts, roaring flames or pale fires, poisons, icy venom that saps one's strength. But Mistilteinn, oh, I think it perhaps the greatest—or most fell—work of this era. For the wounds it inflicts are as real and deadly to immortals as an ordinary sword is to humans."

Starkad bared his teeth—fangs—and jerked his swords free once more. "I'm going to kill you."

A snicker, and then the vampire nigh flew forward, runeblade flashing. Starkad parried. It barely slowed the runeblade, which sliced through his sword. Starkad twisted away and flung the hilt at Tanna. The vampire batted the projectile aside with Mistilteinn.

The problem with making swords of iron instead of worked steel was pure iron was soft. Even a steel-wrought blade could barely stand up to the power of a runeblade. An iron one was hopeless if he needed to parry. Instead, Starkad leapt over Tanna's next blow, landed, and kicked off it.

Tanna swung at him, and Starkad flipped over the vampire to land behind him. The Patriarch's runeblade embedded in the dungeon wall almost a foot deep. Starkad swung at him. Tanna's form brought about to dust. Then came back together as the iron sword seemed to bite into flesh. The vampire staggered backward, hand to his side where Starkad had gouged him deep.

He snarled at Starkad, looked to Mistilteinn, then lunged for Starkad instead. Starkad whipped his sword around once more. Becoming a vampire had made Starkad even faster. Almost as fast as Tanna. Almost.

The other vampire dodged around Starkad's blade, caught his wrist in a steel-like grip, and flung him into the side of the cell. Starkad tried to shift his gravity to the wall the way Arete did, but it came at him too fast and the impact sent his own fangs jamming into his lip. He hit the floor, dazed, but somehow not winded.

Because he didn't breathe except to speak. Huh.

Before he could gain his feet, Tanna was there, his form half solid, half dust. His foot caught Starkad in the ribs and hefted him up so hard Starkad actually hit the ceiling. This time, he did manage to shift his gravity and cling there.

Didn't help, since Tanna leapt up to him an instant later, fist swinging. Starkad rolled to the side and Tanna's fist dented the stone ceiling, sending a spiderweb of cracks along it. Starkad dropped off, hit the floor in a crouch, and lunged for his iron sword. His fingers brushed over the blade on the way to the hilt, and he instantly felt slow and weak.

Claw-like hands dug into his shoulders and sent him crashing against another wall.

Starkad struggled to rise, but pain seeped into every bone in his body. Some of them might well have been cracked. He managed his knees. Twisted to the side as Tanna's fist came in once more. The blow split stone.

Snarling, Starkad landed a hook into Tanna's ribs. The Patriarch barely flinched, instead catching Starkad by the hair and driving him back against the wall. "You, a pathetic neonate, cannot hope to match my power. I am ancient. I feasted on the blood of uncounted souls and grew mighty as I passed down through the ages. I am eternal."

The tip of a blade exploded out of Tanna's chest, driven right through his heart.

"Reckon that means you was immortal, huh?" Höfund said. "'Cause you said this here blade could kill immortals."

The vampire looked down at the runeblade, his hands trembling. Blood spurted from his mouth as an all-too-human expression came over his face.

Starkad sneered at him, slipped around behind the vampire, and took the runeblade's hilt from Höfund. He jerked Mistilteinn free, then hacked off Tanna's head in one swift motion.

The half-jotunn grimaced, backed up into a wall, and wiped blood splatters from his face with one hand, chains still dangling from his wrists. He grunted once, then shook himself. "You figure we can leave Miklagard now?"

"You can." Starkad wiped his own face. "You should."

"You ain't coming?"

"I'm not sure yet ... there are things I need to see to in Tanna's tower."

"Huh. Where's Hervor and the others, then?"

Starkad shook his head. "I don't know. Let's get you out of this place, then you should head to the harbor and see about finding a ship away from here."

The big man pushed off the wall. "Finding a ship is good, sure enough. But I ain't leaving without Hervor."

All Starkad could do was frown.

*a* shadow passed through the night, down the cobbled street, there only for an instant and then gone. Hervor pressed herself hard against the alley wall, uncertain whether the darkness had been her imagination or a vampire stalking the city.

Either way, heading out after dark didn't seem over wise. Not wise, but then, she saw no real alternative. She'd taken one night to rest, but she had to find Starkad, to try to make things right. Or at least to try to help him end Tanna.

Tanna, Orvar, even Starkad now—damn Arete—were like to be out only in the dark hours.

And she had business with all three of them. Poor Win was dead, but she'd given her oath to save Holmgard if she could. Damn oaths, always trapping her.

And she needed to find Orvar-Oddr, too, and Vebiorg, assuming the varulf lived. The latter to gain her help with destroying the former. Hervor would do it alone if she had to, but she liked her odds better with Vebiorg by her side.

So she stalked from alley to alley, watching Tanna's palace and Nikolaos's both. From the gate to Tanna's grounds, a big man stumbled out, steadied himself on the wall, and then shuffled onward.

Höfund?

Oh, praise Odin. Hervor had begun to think the Ás king had utterly abandoned them all here.

Glancing both ways down the road—and seeing no sign of vampires or draugar—she hurried toward him.

The half-jotunn drew up short at her approach, squinted, then stomped toward her and threw his arms around her. "Half feared you was dead."

She could hardly breathe with him squeezing her so tight, but she struggled to return his embrace. "Same."

Höfund released her, wobbled, and she caught him. He weighed more than most men, so even his arm around her shoulder nigh bore her down. Still, by the look of him, he'd fared even worse than her. Wounds everywhere, feet burned to a crisp. The poor bastard was barely alive, from what she could tell.

"What happened?"

"Orvar tortured me, here and there. Figuring on hurting you by hurting your crew, I reckon. That, and Tanna and his creatures took to drinking my blood more oft than I'd have liked, if anyone bothered to ask on it."

Hervor grimaced. "How did you get away?"

"Eightarms came in, fought with Tanna. We killed him, but Starkad just disappeared off into the night saying that things in the tower needed tending to. Dunno for sure, but I reckon maybe he meant Orvar." Höfund wheezed, leaning more heavily upon her shoulder. "Told him we ought all best be sailing off, but he's a right stubborn one, that."

Truer words had never been said.

Hervor guided the big man away, toward an alley. "Starkad was right here?"

"Was, but I can't say as he's like to still be close. He was moving a bit faster than I could manage, truth be told."

Shit. Hel take all vampires, Starkad included. "You truly killed Tanna?"

The big man chuckled, a deep rumbling sound that might've been intimidating, if his mirth wasn't so damned good-natured. Like he was also so eager to share his joviality. "Ran him right through with his own blade, I did. Don't normally hold with stabbing a man in the back, but I reckon he had it coming, all in all."

"I'd say he did." And one problem solved, at least. Starkad and Höfund had upheld their oaths to Rollaugr, though the king might rather have had his son returned to him. He'd have to take whatever small satisfaction victory offered him, though. Naught else remained to any of them.

She helped Höfund to the alley, and then he leaned on a building, the release of weight from her shoulder drawing a sigh from her. The big man was staring at her now, as if waiting for her to tell him what to do next. Maybe once she'd been the captain of a crew, but honestly, she'd been a rather evil bitch back then.

And again, in Pohjola, well, she'd all but murdered Ecgtheow, gotten almost all the rest of her crew killed, and somehow failed to foresee Wudga's betrayal despite knowing she ought to trust him less than a godsdamned troll. No, she didn't really need to be in charge of aught. And yet, here was Höfund, looking at her and waiting for her to say something to make everything all better.

She leaned with her back against the wall herself. So her oath to Rollaugr was fulfilled, true, but she had to try to keep her oath to Starkad. And either way, she had to see to Orvar. That bastard needed to die. Or she did. Either way, she'd had her fill of him and she'd made her decision to stop running.

"Got something deep rumbling around in that head of yours, I reckon."

Naught good. She looked back to the half-jotunn. Hurt as he was, he'd probably come with her if she asked. And he'd die for it. Orvar would make certain of that. No, too many people had died over her crime.

Höfund might well be the closest thing to a good man she'd ever met. Enough so she didn't want him to wind up the way everyone else in her life did, anyway.

"I need you to do something for me."

He shrugged, then grimaced as even that little motion had pained him.

"Can you make it alone to the harbor?" She pointed off in the direction of the Black Sea.

Höfund sucked his teeth. "Been through worse than this."

That seemed doubtful, but she'd have to take it as his way of telling her not to worry over him. Which, considering she had rather enough to fret on at the moment, she'd have to accept. "Go to the harbor, staying out of sight as you make your way. At dawn, find a ship willing to carry us out of Miklagard. Have them wait for me as long as they can, an hour from sunset if they'll do so." Hervor fished out one of the pouches of silver they'd stolen from Tanna's vaults and pressed it into Höfund's hands. "If I'm not back by then, I'm not coming back. And you need to go, take the ship and go."

The big man shoved the pouch half inside his trousers, but frowned and shook his head. "Ain't leaving without you."

She fought down the smile his stubborn loyalty almost

brought to her face. "Listen to me. I have to go after Orvar. You're in no state to aid me now." He opened his mouth, but she talked right over him. "No. You know it's the truth. You come along you're more like to get me killed than help me. But I cannot allow this to go on. I must deal with my mistakes. Vebiorg will aid me." Assuming the varulf even lived. "But I cannot do what I need to do if part of me fears you're about to do something blisteringly foolish like charging in to rescue me. So I want your ..." And here it came, back to this. Always back to it. "I want your oath, Höfund. If I do not return before the last tide of the day, you get on the ship and sail from this place."

"I ain't giving no such oath."

Hervor grimaced. Stubborn bastard was nigh as bad as Starkad. And she would not be responsible for his death. No more. She slapped Höfund.

The big man backed away, hand to his check, mouth gaping.

"Your godsdamned pride is like to get us both killed. Give me your oath!"

The half-jotunn spat on the cobbles, glared at her a moment. "You want it so much, fine. I give you my oath. I'll leave on the last tide. So you'd best be there too."

Hervor nodded, trying to keep her face looking hopeful, as much for her benefit as his. With any luck, she and Starkad and Vebiorg would all be on that ship with Höfund.

But Hervor hadn't been much favored by luck of late.

## 30

The corpses of men and vampires lay strewn around Tanna's tower. Blood splattered the walls, dripped down from the ceiling, and coated nigh every floor in the place. And Starkad was not yet finished. He'd worked his way to the top, slaughtering everyone he could find loyal to the fallen Patriarch.

None of it sated his rage. And so he delved into the hidden basements beneath the tower, killed a man smoking a hookah, and cut through Tanna's collection of semi-clad and naked women in the room beyond. Some few of them were vampires, but most human. Starkad paused his slaughter only to sate his thirst on one.

The room was decorated with plush pillows, several heated pools, and numerous alcoves. Fluted columns supported the chamber, which seemed wider than the entire tower. Torches on those columns illuminated Tanna's collection of whores.

Except whores got paid.

Maybe Tanna was not to blame for all the wretched urd that had unfolded in recent days. Still, his invasion of Holmgard had sparked this conflagration, and Starkad aimed to make certain no other Patriarch wished to repeat such folly.

Besides, he had something to see to here. Some things could not be borne without recompense.

From an alcove, a vampire dropped from the ceiling, snarling as he tried to ram twin knives into Starkad's throat. Mistilteinn split his skull down the middle.

The women had been screaming from the moment he started his grim mission. As a mortal man, he'd never have stomached such a massacre. Now, sickening as it was, the blood was almost as arousing as the exposed flesh.

He came around the column to see Afrid Stonekicker, clad only with a sheer sheet around her waist and naught at all over her chest. Along with two other women, she was crouched back in an alcove. The others cowered behind her, looking pathetic compared to the corded muscles on Afrid's arms and her defined abdomen.

Starkad snickered. "I suspected I could find you in this tower. Even I did not realize this was how Tanna would repay your service."

Afrid drew her chin up, the little defiance spoiled by the slight tremble in her lip and the whimpering of the women behind her.

Starkad growled at the three of them, baring his fangs. Even Afrid fell back a step, hit the pillowed benches lining the alcove, and had nowhere else to go. That drew a snicker from him. "So you whored yourself to your enemy for a few days' more life." Starkad shook his head. "Or did he promise you immortality?"

The sound of her pounding heart, luscious and terrifying, made clear Tanna had not fulfilled any such promise, had he even offered it.

"What do you want?"

He chuckled. "I have to wonder where we'd be if you had not betrayed us. Maybe things would've worked out much the same. The unfolding of urd will not be denied. Your fate, too, seems inevitable."

Afrid moaned, ever so slightly. "What are you going to do to me?"

"How does he take you, whore? In the pools? Do you get on your hands and knees? Does he use the couches?"

Afrid flinched with each word. Shit, maybe Tanna and his men had tried all of the above. "Is that what you want?" Her voice sounded nigh to breaking. Pathetic. The once proud shieldmaiden broken by the horrors of the Otherworlds. "You can have me any way you want. Take me from here, and I'll ... I'll pleasure you every day. I'll be your slave!"

Starkad couldn't help but frown to see a warrior so fallen. Destroyed, body and soul, by forces she could not have imagined dwelt here. Nor could she have hoped to have survived them. Still, she could've died with some courage, same as Baruch or Fjolvor or Tveggi. Maybe more of the crew, too, Starkad wasn't sure. He didn't know what had become of Win or Vebiorg, or even Hervor now.

He drew in a breath and blew it out. He didn't require breath, of course, but the motion was so ingrained it still served to help calm him, focus his thoughts. "I came here to kill you. The only thing I desired from you was vengeance."

Afrid closed her eyes tight, raised her throat, and then stared defiantly at him. "Then just do it. Be done with it."

Starkad sneered at the fallen shieldmaiden. "Seeing you so pathetic, I find you not worth the killing. Go. Run from here and escape the city if you can." He almost couldn't believe his own words. All this slaughter and he'd been thinking of finding Afrid and avenging her betrayal. But then, he'd never imagined finding a naked, abused young girl.

The shieldmaiden stared at him with such fury he half expected her to attack him, try to force him into giving her some semblance of an honorable death. Maybe he would if she tried it. Instead, she edged around him, followed by the other two, then made a break for the entrance.

"So," a hollow, ghostly voice said from the shadows.

Starkad snarled as he turned.

Orvar-Oddr had caught Afrid by the throat and hefted her off the ground. One of the draug's arms was severed at the elbow and one of his legs was a ruined mess Starkad found hard to believe even supported his weight. "All this, and you find mercy in your heart for the very wretch who betrayed you."

The girl wriggled, arms flailing uselessly against the draug. Her cheeks had begun to take on a slight bluish tinge. Starkad almost pitied her. But letting her go was a far cry from doing aught to save her.

Orvar actually grinned. Unlike a vampire, a draug had pronounced canines on the top and bottom of his mouth. Almost made a bite from the creature seem worse. "I admit —I am shocked to see you survive Tyrfing's venom. I would've thought it impossible even for you. And able to speak again? Never."

"I didn't survive."

"No, I suppose you didn't. Neither of us did. Ironic, I suppose. That bitch shieldmaiden killed us both, led us both to this wretched unlife, and with the very same weapon."

Starkad nodded. "I have no quarrel with you. We were friends for long years."

Orvar snickered, squeezed his hand tighter until even

the faintest of thrashing went out of Afrid. Then he tossed her corpse aside. "While you lived, I hated you with blinding passion, as I hated all my former crew. All life. Dead, I find you almost tolerable. Why is that?"

"We have no quarrel, you and I," Starkad repeated.

"Oh, perhaps not. But the *other* shieldmaiden yet lives, and your death will hurt her worse than aught else. Unfortunately, I see no alternative but to put an end to your suffering." Orvar drew a sword from over his shoulder.

Starkad shook his head and drew Mistilteinn. "I don't wish to fight you. Believe me when I tell you, you do not wish to fight me. You are maimed, and I carry a sword that can slay even ghosts such as us."

Orvar stalked forward, shaking his head. "You're right. I don't truly wish to fight you. But I have no choice. I have to end this. My very nature compels it. In the end, we have few choices in our lives, if any. Even fewer in death."

The choking grasp of urd. Orvar clearly felt it too, crushing him. And the draug was obviously in no state to be denied.

Starkad bared his teeth. And he charged in, runeblade gleaming in the torchlight.

## 31

The main door to Tanna's tower had been cleaved through and kicked in. Beyond, the carnage started in earnest. Bodies cleft in twain, so many severed limbs and heads Hervor couldn't even judge how many men and women had fallen here. The halls stank of blood and shit, the odor so powerful it churned her gut.

Everywhere she looked, people and vampires were eviscerated and hewed to pieces. If Starkad had done this alone, he had reached a new level of destructive capability. It looked more like a whirlwind of blades had swept through the tower, passing up and down the stairs and leaving naught but viscera strewn in its wake.

Hand to her mouth at the overpowering reek—to say naught of the awful sight—Hervor stalked back down the first flight of stairs. Where was everyone?

A pair of barely clad women ran shrieking from the tower's basement, glanced at Hervor and the chaos, and bolted for the main door. So he'd gone below, then.

Hervor charged down those stairs, allowing a few other

naked whores to escape around her only because she couldn't otherwise get past them. The screams echoed from beyond a satin curtain. She threw this back and came into a recently abandoned chamber thick with reeking smoke and oil fumes. The fleeing women had overturned tables and cushions, leaving broken ceramics littering the floor, no doubt from one of those strange pipes the smoke billowed out of.

What in Odin's stones was this? Who would possibly suck smoke into their lungs on purpose?

The clang of metal on metal rang out from behind the next curtain, so Hervor charged through that as well and out into a larger chamber, this one strewn with small pools and pillow-lined alcoves. The room where the naked women had been?

Orvar was there, slashing at Starkad, who parried attack after attack, offering his own offense only weakly and on rare occasions. Starkad still didn't want to kill him, but Orvar seemed to have no problem slaying Hervor's former lover.

Which wasn't going to happen. She jerked Tyrfing free and charged in, growling.

Orvar spun, keeping both of them in view. "Finally. I was beginning to think she wasn't coming. I could hardly begin the last verse of this warped tale without all the players."

"Just shut up!" Hervor roared. She swiped Tyrfing at him.

Orvar knocked her blade aside with ease, danced around her, grinning with those hateful fangs of his. "Would you begrudge me the end you yourself have wrought? All of your lies and betrayals, your very own actions guiding us ever toward this culmination of urd?"

"I don't want to kill you ..." Starkad said.

Orvar chuckled, even the sound making Hervor cringe. "Nor can we stay locked in eternal combat as though this were some poorly conceived tale of gods and heroes. For we are none of us either of those things, are we?"

"If you can't do it, Starkad," Hervor said, "then I will."

Growling, shaking his head, Starkad did fall back a step.

Orvar snickered again, bringing his sword up. The loss of half an arm seemed to bother him little, though his savaged leg did give him a slight limp. Nevertheless, he whipped his sword around in masterful arcs that forced Hervor to give ground.

Maybe Tyrfing would've made up for him being more skilled than her—especially considering she had to fight left-handed—but naught accounted for him being stronger, faster, and having unending stamina.

Still, she'd told Starkad she'd do this herself. And she had one thing going for her. One area she could finally match Orvar.

*Rage.*

Shrieking, Hervor slammed Tyrfing against Orvar's blade, whipped it back at his face. The runeblade tore through the putrid remains of the draug's cheek, and he turned his head aside for an instant. Hervor spun her blade around to thrust, but Orvar knocked Tyrfing aside and brought his knee up into her gut.

The blow sent her staggering back only to crash into one of the pools. The water might've been waist-deep, but on her arse, it rushed up over her head. She scrambled for the surface, barely held on to Tyrfing, and brought the blade up, expecting to get her head cleaved in two in the process.

But the draug had backed away, toward the entrance to

this chamber, chuckling. Drawing it out. Actually enjoying all this?

Fuck it. If he wanted to enjoy his vengeance, then so would she. Soaked, she trudged out of the pool and stomped over toward the draug, Tyrfing clasped in both hands. "I will end you this night."

Another mind-grating chuckle. "Perhaps. But you two shall accompany me through the gates of Hel."

Starkad groaned, but Hervor couldn't well spare the time to look at him.

Instead, she charged Orvar once more, whipping Tyrfing around in a savage arc.

Orvar dodged behind a column, and her runeblade cleaved through a torch sconce wedged into the stone column and held fast. Oh, Odin's hairy stones! Hervor placed a foot on the column and heaved, knowing Orvar might come around the column any moment. But without the runeblade, she was already fucking dead, so what did it matter?

Except the draug hadn't closed in on her. Indeed, he'd stooped to snatch up the fallen torch, holding it awkwardly in the same hand as his sword. "It struck me some time ago that you might come here in the end. And after what happened in that ruined temple, well, I imagined a most fitting end to our saga."

"You truly talk too much," Hervor said. Tyrfing lurched free and she stumbled backward several steps.

"Oh ... but you'll want to hear this. And while I did not imagine Starkad would live, it does seem fitting he too should join us here at the end. Urd bound the three of us together. If any tell our tale, they will say how we lived and died, close as lovers."

"What are you on about?" Starkad said, his voice coming from Hervor's left. Orvar's strange words must've drawn him in.

"Your whore has surprised me with her tenacity. Her ability to survive and overcome one perilous challenge after the next. I would've been a fool to think she could not have made it here." Orvar shrugged. "Besides, if I did kill her, what would I have to make my wretched existence worthwhile? Servitude to a vampire Patriarch?" He sneered. "Not so appealing." He flung the torch not at Hervor, but at the curtain separating this room from the smoking chamber.

The fabric ignited as if it were fresh kindling and Hervor stumbled away from the sudden inferno. "You soaked the curtains in oil?"

The draug chuckled again.

The blaze brushed against the walls, and even the stone caught fire, a line of flame shooting around the perimeter of the room and igniting alcove after alcove. Pillows ignited into blazes, the satin drapery becoming a conflagration.

"Oil?" Orvar said. "They call it liquid fire."

An explosion rocked the smoking room—the only gods-damned exit—with enough force Hervor pitched over onto her arse. The scorching wind tore the curtain to pieces, those flaming fragments landing on the ground. Streams of fire shot along the chamber in winding arcs, as if Orvar had poured this foulness almost at random.

Hervor scrambled away from the spreading blaze, regained her feet, and found flames had leapt up between her and Orvar. No sign of Starkad.

"You see, the Patriarchs have barrels and barrels of this stuff stored to fight off Serklander invasions," Orvar said. "They fling it at ships from great contraptions you wouldn't believe. Smells like oil, but then, the stench of hookah smoke rather covers that up."

Heat washed over Hervor's face as the blaze continued to leap around the room, spreading in all directions. Everywhere she turned, the flames rose up. How the fuck did stone burn?

"So," Orvar said, deftly stalked around a curving line of flame, sword in hand as he closed in on her. "I don't really have to kill you now. Just stop you from getting out. Shouldn't be overly difficult considering the way out is on fire. On the other hand ... running you through might offer some satisfaction."

The draug lunged at her. Hervor fell back. Fire singed her arse, forcing her forward, and she barely got Tyrfing up to parry Orvar's overhand chop. He rained down another blow, and another, driving back, almost into the flames.

Orvar bellowed a feral war cry, swinging down again. Hervor's arm—already numb—gave out and she pitched over sideways. Her left hand landed in the flames and squelched in the oil-like jelly. Fire leapt up her arm. Red agony nigh blinded her. She was only dimly aware of her own screams. She stumbled from the flames, shrieking, toppled into the pool and splashed under water.

It took her a heartbeat, face under the now warm water, to realize the fire was still burning her. Underwater. Hervor screamed again, sucking down a lungful of water, burst through the surface to be struck by the sound of Orvar's maddening cackles ringing out through the chamber.

She knew she was wailing but couldn't stop. The fire just kept burning her. It brushed from her arm up her neck, scorching her left cheek.

Splashing through the pool, shrieking in pain and

horror, she scrambled as far from the flames as she could. That meant away from the exit.

Because Orvar was right. He didn't need to kill her. The growing smoke and endless flames would do that. And she had no way out, even if she could get past the draug.

His cackles reached her even over the sound of her own agonized screaming.

## 32

Clouds of black smoke filled the room and obscured Starkad's vision, bringing back sickening memories of his visions of Muspelheim. The smoke here was rising toward the high ceiling, but the longer the fires raged, the more of it came toward ground level. And those fires showed no signs of slowing.

Lines of it divided him from Orvar as well as from the pool where Hervor was shrieking. He could get to neither of them. After the way the oil from the fire had clung to Hervor's hand, he dare not try to dash through it either.

The draug just kept laughing, twirling his sword in front of the exit as the whole room blazed around him.

Starkad spun, taking in every possible option. Flames had sectioned off the room, though, and he saw no way past unless he could fly.

Fly ...

Arete had walked on walls. And Starkad had clung to the ceiling for an instant when fighting Tanna. Sections of the walls were aflame too, but it seemed Orvar had been even more haphazard in coating the walls with the liquid fire than he had on the floor.

Starkad raced to the nearest wall and put a foot on it. Naught happened. Damn it. He needed an edge. Something to get him past this. He needed to be on the fucking wall. All of a sudden, he felt the world around him lurch, as if down suddenly became the vertical surface. He stumbled up, his other foot no longer having purchase on the ground.

Orvar had stopped laughing. The draug stared at him, fangs bared.

Starkad raced up the wall, arm raised against the thickening smoke. He couldn't see much. It took him a moment to remember he didn't actually need to breathe, though. He charged through the darkness, then shifted onto the ceiling and raced in the general direction he'd seen Orvar.

As far as he knew, no part of the ceiling was actually on fire. If it was, he was in for an unfortunate surprise. Trying to stay as silent as possible under the circumstances, he ran until he was fair certain Orvar was beneath him.

Then he leapt straight up toward the ground and imagined it as down. He spun around in midair and landed in a crouch a few feet in front of Orvar.

The draug scrambled back, sword raised and shaking his head. "Well ... I suppose as long as Hervor and I are dead, it matters less if you survive."

"I didn't want to kill you."

"You and I are both already dead." Orvar sneered. "Nor does peace lie before either of us when our bodies perish. We are ghosts now, and losing our corpses is but losing our hosts so that we must wander, lost and damned through the shadows. Eternal torment is our legacy."

Starkad grimaced, shook his head. "Why? Why did you have to bring us to this?"

"Ask that bitch you spent so many years fucking." Orvar lunged at him, maybe even faster than he'd been in life.

Not fast enough. Starkad batted the draug's sword away with Mistilteinn. He could've probably run Orvar through then and there. But his blade wouldn't quite move. Damn it.

Damn Orvar. Damn Hervor. Damn fucking Odin for bringing Starkad to this life.

Damn ... urd itself.

He roared, slashing at Orvar's head. The draug ducked, his kick sending Starkad stumbling back, close enough that flames singed his arse.

Orvar grinned. "Oh. That is wonderful. You cannot do it. You cannot bring yourself to kill me. And that being the case, I'm going to kill you. The sheer, beautiful irony of it is ... delicious. I will savor your death almost as much as hers."

"No." Starkad brought Mistilteinn up once more, waving it before him. "No. You are going to end here. This cannot go on. Not after all you have wrought."

The draug came in swinging low, forcing Starkad into an awkward parry. Orvar spun around, whipping his sword toward Starkad's neck.

In a single motion, Starkad ducked, lunged forward, and thrust Mistilteinn up. The runeblade bit through Orvar's heart and punched out his back, stealing all strength from the draug's intended blow. His sword clattered uselessly from his hand and he stared down at the runeblade embedded in his chest. The draug grunted, teeth bared.

Strange to think the creature's heart did not even beat, and yet, somehow, this sword through it had affected Orvar the same as if he'd been alive. Starkad's old friend wrapped a hand around Mistilteinn's blade, heedless of how it cut his palm.

He stared at Starkad. And slowly, the red gleam went out of his eyes.

So it was done.

He ought to have felt more. Despite the raging flames all around him, Starkad just felt cold. He'd killed one more person he'd claimed to love. In life, those murders had haunted him, chasing him down through the years. Literally, in Ogn's case, but the others real, just the same. This one, though, it only felt ... hollow.

Urd had brought him here and left him with no choices at all. He jerked Mistilteinn free from his friend's rotten, disfigured corpse. The real Orvar-Oddr had died years ago in Thule. As long as Starkad kept telling himself that, maybe Orvar would never become another shade haunting his dreams.

Hervor's groans of pain tore through Starkad's reverie. The shieldmaiden had crawled from the pool, Tyrfing clutched in her right hand. The other hand had become a charred, blackened mess. Deep, blistering burns oozing blood had spread up her arm, her neck, and onto her cheek, marring her exotic beauty.

A wall of fire separated them, but she was staring at him now, arm clutched tight to her chest, face a mask of pain. Staring at him, as if begging him for something.

But Starkad had naught left. Naught for Hervor, naught even for himself. Maybe it would be better if he just stayed here and burned, alongside Hervor and Orvar-Oddr's corpse. Let everything vanish in the flames, just as the tormented draug had intended. A fitting end to a sick tale and a wretched life lived too long.

Except Starkad had been willing to take Arete's offer for another moment of life. For immortality so long denied him. And having sacrificed so very much along the way for it, he could hardly cast it aside.

Hervor had not moved, was still watching his face. Maybe knowing he was going to leave her here to burn. It was the urd she had wrought for herself, well-earned.

Hel, Hervor herself must know that. She didn't plead, didn't make a sound save her grunts of pain. Even if she got out of here, she might well die of burns like that.

Let her burn ... Let her become one more ghost in the long stream of those he'd left behind.

Fitting.

Starkad turned, made his way to the wall and climbed up it. He would leave all Miklagard behind. Arete might try to stop him, might even come looking for him. The vampire woman seemed to think she had some claim on him for having made him immortal. Starkad felt otherwise.

He walked up the wall, back into the smoke clogging the ceiling. Hervor disappeared from his view as did almost all else.

Leaving her to burn was justice ... was maybe even the right thing to do. But then, neither of those things had truly driven most of Starkad's actions thus far. Much as he loathed her for all she'd done, he could not deny the memories of their years together.

"I love you." Her voice was almost a whisper, like maybe she thought he was already gone and now was saying what she no longer dared speak to his face.

Indeed, had she had the temerity to make such a brazen claim, Starkad might well have struck her down. But hearing now, knowing it wasn't even meant for his ears, it felt like a lance through his own lifeless heart.

Hel take her.

He dropped down from the ceiling and landed behind her.

She was on her knees, coughing, choking on the smoke. Tyrfing clutched in her right hand, almost like she'd considered turning it on herself. Maybe a better end than burning in the flames.

With a grimace, Starkad sheathed Mistilteinn.

Hervor slowly turned toward him, mouth agape, but—wisely—saying naught.

Starkad hefted her up and threw her over his shoulder, then worked his way back to a section of the wall free of flames. He probably couldn't shift her center of gravity to the wall, but he had the strength to hold her despite that. He stepped up on the wall and started upward. No clear path to the hookah room.

"Hold your breath and close your eyes."

He raced up into the billowing smoke that covered the ceiling, having no alternative. She wouldn't last long up here. Starkad stepped onto the ceiling, then ran in the direction of the hookah lounge. At the far wall, he dropped down.

The room before him was engulfed in a blaze worse than the harem, and the ceiling was lower, that aflame as well. But it was the oil that presented the biggest threat. That was what wouldn't go out. So if he could pass through the room without actually getting the oil on either of them ...

It would hurt. It would hurt a lot.

"Take a deep breath," he told her, then shifted her into his arms, cradled like a babe but held slightly higher, just below his chin. Above most of the flames.

He saw no other way.

Starkad spat. Then he took off at a dead run, not even

bothering trying to avoid the flames. His feet squelched in the oil—more like jelly, actually—so it no doubt covered his boots. The conflagration ignited his trousers and seared his legs.

He passed through the room in an instant though, toppled to the ground, and rolled, Hervor tumbling from his arms and slamming against the stairs. Growling at the pain, Starkad jerked off his boots and flung them aside, then tore off the ends of his trousers and patted out what flames he could. His legs were charred black as bad as Hervor's arm.

Snarling, he lay back, unable to even think of walking.

"Starkad," Hervor said, crawling over to him. "You saved me ..."

He looked at her, teeth grit through the agony, though she must have felt even worse.

She reached for his arm. "I can help you up the stairs. We have to get out of here."

Starkad shoved her away. "Go."

"No! I won't leave without you."

A fresh grunt of pain escaped him. He turned to stare dead into her eyes. "I will not have your hands upon my flesh, you lying, murderous wretch. I am done with you, forever." She flinched at each word, her mouth hanging open. "I have no wish to ever look upon your face again. And believe me when I tell you, you do *not* wish to see me again. Take what remains of your life ... and be gone. Before hunger takes me."

Starkad couldn't remember ever seeing tears in Hervor's eyes before. Maybe now, as she knelt there, silently working her jaw ... maybe it was just the smoke and the pain watering her eyes. She reached a trembling hand toward him, then let it fall.

Finally, she rose, grasped Tyrfing, and disappeared up the stairs.

Starkad waited until he was certain she was gone.

And then he wailed as despair closed in around his woeful soul.

## 33

*G*iven all that had happened, Hervor had dared not delay until daylight to be free of Miklagard. Even without the threat of vampires prowling the streets, she could not have stomached the city another moment.

So she and Höfund had stolen a tiny sailing vessel and set out, skirting the coast west of the city. Like this, she could not have said how long it would take to reach Holmgard. Nor did she really care.

It was hard to care much about aught anymore.

A lump of solid ice had grown inside her heart, and it was spreading, seeping into her gut. Filling up her lungs and choking out her breath. Stealing her ability to speak or even to think.

Despite the burns covering her arm and neck and up her face, she was freezing.

She guided the ship, hardly noticing the pain in her left hand, though she could only steer with her right hand now. She hardly even heard Höfund as he spoke. Naught he could've said much mattered, anyway.

It was over.

Everything was over.

She'd ... avenged her father and uncles back on Thule. It had been blood calling out for blood. Justice, as her kin deserved. Vengeance ...

All that had motivated Orvar-Oddr ever since. The Arrow's Point had nigh drowned in his need for vengeance. He'd stalked around Midgard, slaughtered Odin alone knew how many people along the way.

Cost her ... cost her ...

The ice in her chest just kept growing. By the time they reached Holmgard, maybe she'd have frozen solid. It would've been fitting if she never returned. In Miklagard, she'd lived her greatest fear. Starkad had learned everything.

It had destroyed them.

That last look upon his face had made the truth unavoidably clear.

"You're looking pale."

Hervor glanced at Höfund, still only half-seeing the big man. That ice just kept crushing her. Slow and cold and inevitable. Just like Orvar's revenge. She'd killed him now. And he'd still fucking won. "I'm all right."

"Sure?"

Hervor didn't answer. She didn't have the strength to lie, and she sure as Odin's stones didn't have the strength to tell him the truth. Chills wracked her.

She didn't have the strength for much of aught.

The ice had stolen away her strength and left a numbness in its place. Left a part of her to wish the draug had killed her.

She'd killed him a second time.

And she'd still lost.

Finally, she could stop looking over her shoulder. Only now there was naught ahead of her worth looking at.

### ❧

AN EERIE SILENCE had settled over her grandfather's hall, a stillness that Hervor misliked even before she rapped on the doors. Waited.

No one answered.

Hervor glanced over her shoulder at Höfund.

"Sure you've got the right place?"

Hervor rolled her eyes. Was he truly asking if she'd forgotten which lands had belonged to her family? She shouldered a door only to find it didn't budge. Barred from the inside. Since when did Grandfather bar the damn doors?

Her left hand was still wrapped in reeking bandages a völva had applied. Saved her life, maybe. She'd probably never use that hand again, though.

"Open up!" she demanded, rapping hard once more. "Open up! This is my godsdamned home!"

"Lady Hervor?" a voice called from within, muffled by the thick oak separating them, but clearly female.

"Yes! Is that you, Toril? Let me in, damn it! Night is settling in."

Groaning sounded behind the door, along with wood scraping, then clattering to the floor. Poor girl could probably barely lift the plank needed to seal the double doors. To spare the servant the effort, Hervor shoved the doors open herself.

Toril scampered away like trolls were stomping through

instead of Hervor, the servant's face ashen, wan. "S-sorry, I … times have been hard of late. Too many men poking around looking for …" The woman was staring at Hervor's face, no doubt afraid to ask about the burns running along her neck and up her cheek, or the bandaged lump of a hand Hervor held to her chest. Not that Hervor would've answered, anyway.

"What happened here?" Hervor demanded. "Where's Grandfather?"

Toril hesitated, removing any remaining doubt. "Thickness finally took him, not a moon after you left."

And that ice just kept growing inside her chest. Hervor groaned, leaned against the wall. Höfund put a hand on her shoulder and she shrugged it off. She hadn't been there when Mother died. Hadn't even seen her fall ill. Now Grandfather was gone too, and she hadn't been here because she'd gone chasing after wealth in Miklagard. Chasing after Starkad.

Like a fool. Because she ought to have known it wouldn't end well. Naught had ever really ended well for her.

*The gods are watching, little girl. They watch while you fumble around in the dark.*

A völva had said that to her, back before she went to Samsey. Before she took Tyrfing from Angantyr's barrow. Before everything turned to troll shit. The witch had claimed Hervor was too stubborn to listen to wisdom freely given.

Teeth grit, Hervor stood there, chuckling, not caring as Toril and Höfund stared at her like she'd gone mist-mad. Because of course she had. She'd gone mist-mad long, long ago. Maybe when she left Grandfather's care and took up with Red-Eye's Boys. Certainly after that, when she'd sworn vengeance upon Orvar-Oddr for crimes committed before she was born against men she'd never even known.

Pride? Arrogance. Hubris. Sheer, rank stupidity.

She'd taken the sword from the barrow, despite the ghost's warnings.

*You tread swiftly toward your own doom. You walk in darkness.*

Odin's thrice-damned stones ... Her father had known her oath would lead her to despair. He'd known. He'd fucking told her.

*Tyrfing will be the ruin of all your family.*

"Agh!" Hervor pressed her palms into her eyes, even that sending fresh pain through her left hand. "Agh!"

"Hervor!" Höfund had her shoulders, was shaking her.

Teeth clenched and bared, she stared at him, knowing she must look mad and not giving a troll's rocky arse about it. "I did it. I upheld my oath! I upheld my oath!" She slapped the big man's arm. "I fulfilled it! So why? Why!" Why hadn't she listened? Why hadn't she stopped for even a moment ...

But then, her oath had brought her to Starkad in the first place. Brought them together, given them a chance. A fool's chance, an illusion born on mist and carried across the night to draw men to their doom. Hope was a will-o'-the-wisp, and she'd willingly chased it into a bog.

Maybe she deserved all she'd gotten from it.

"Hervor?"

She rolled her eyes, then finally stared at him. Grandfather was gone. All her family was gone. And the last thing he'd asked her ...

*Hervor ... you are the last of our line. If you ...*

If she did not bear a child, both lines of her family

ended with her. All her oaths of vengeance meant less than naught. Maybe Angantyr's ghost rested now, but his kin were gone, save her.

And Grandfather had asked her to marry Höfund. Son of a king, if a foreign one. Grandfather hadn't known what manner of king Godmund was, but maybe that mattered little now. Maybe naught mattered overmuch anymore.

She could not force either a smile or a frown to her face. Couldn't find the strength to break through the ice for even one more breath. "Before he died, Grandfather bid me accept your offer for my hand. If you still wish it ..."

Höfund nodded, cracking a grin wide enough for the both of them. "Can't say aught would make me happier. Reckon I'll use some of this plundered silver in the town, work up a proper celebration."

For his sake, Hervor faked a smile. He deserved so much more, but that was all she had left to offer. A pathetic smile, and a heart of ice.

In the morning, the townsfolk would gather for the wedding. Hervor had no kin to gather, and Höfund's lay far beyond Midgard, so instead he'd invited people neither of them knew nor cared for.

Hervor walked in the hills outside Grandfather's estate, alone. Höfund had asked to come with her, of course, worried over her heading out into the mist at night. But she'd taken a torch and Tyrfing and refused any company. Some things had to be done alone. Maybe, in the end, everything that mattered was done alone.

A fell wind whipped the mist into swirls that seemed wicked, as if watching her. Though it prickled her skin, still she could not bring herself to fear. Not anymore. She should have, perhaps, but after all she'd been through, the night held no more terror. Or Hervor had no capacity left to feel it.

She plodded out through Deeppine, down paths she'd walked back with Red-Eye's Boys long years before. They were all dead now. All the bandits. All of Grandfather's men who had hunted and killed the gang, for that matter. Everyone was gone.

When she was with them, just a girl really, they had come to rocks by the river, where awful whispers filtered up through gaps between the stones. A hole that led down to the gates of Hel, Red-Eye had said. They'd all warned her to stay clear of there, especially at night. Said ghosts clawed their way out to feast on the souls of the unwary.

Once, when a man had turned on him, betrayed him, Red-Eye had broken the traitor's legs and cast him down that hateful hole. That was what happened to traitors and oathbreakers, he'd said. Cast down toward Hel's domain, to be feasted upon by the dark dragon.

Hervor climbed up along the rocks until she could stare down into the darkness of that hole. The torchlight failed to illuminate the bottom though it reflected off numerous boulders lining the way down.

Almost as if aware of her intent, Tyrfing began to sing in her mind. A whisper, a cry for blood and glory, as if she could claim all she would ever desire with its pale flame in hand. But all Hervor desired was forever denied to her.

Soon, the sun would rise, and she'd don a dress and marry Höfund. Bear him a child or several, continue the line. Give over the life of a shieldmaiden which had brought Hervor naught but misery, really. Mother had wanted her to live as a lady, and Hervor had scorned her. Had embraced blood and violence as both means and end.

Fool that she'd always been.

No more, though. She would wed Höfund and force herself to bury thoughts of Starkad Eightarms deep in this hole, to be considered rarely, if ever.

*Tyrfing will be the ruin of all your family.*

She chuckled, shaking her head. Arngrim had murdered Sigrlami and taken this blade. With it, her father Angantyr had wrought chaos and death—most of all his own, leading to Arngrim's suicide. And Angantyr had *warned* her. Told her exactly what would happen.

Oh, but they could be glorious together. They could reclaim all she had lost. Build their own kingdom ... Fuck, were those thoughts even her own? And if not, how many of her thoughts over the years had come from the cursed blade? Had it stoked her need for vengeance, forced her hand?

Or was blaming the sword merely a cowardly way to shift responsibility from herself? Of course, she already knew the answer to that.

Eyes closed, Hervor unslung the runeblade from her shoulder, held the sheathed weapon in her left hand. It was a part of her now. Like one of her own limbs. To let it go was impossible.

Impossible ... A well of despair and madness ...

But Hervor had given in to madness some time ago.

*Tyrfing will be the ruin of all your family.*

And she had not listened. Not when her father had tried to tell her. Not then, not until she could share his wretched agony.

"Let it be done ..." She swallowed, unable to get the lump in her throat down. No. No! She couldn't do this. She needed to put the strap back on her shoulder. To keep Tyrfing close. It was *hers*. Only for her ... "Goodbye my love."

Choking, Hervor forced her fingers open, one by one, each more painful and difficult than the last. Until Tyrfing slipped from her hands.

The runeblade fell into the hole, clattered off stone, bounced, and vanished, into the darkness.

# EPILOGUE

*T*oo many battles had taken their toll upon Odin. His immortal body would heal, yes, but between the loss of vitality he'd suffered fighting in Miklagard and the injuries the Niflungar had inflicted upon him, he found riding Sleipnir sent painful jolts through his body.

The eight-legged horse could cover great distances very quickly, even running over the sea. At least when Odin could tolerate the jarring of such speeds. Now, he found himself preferring a gentler pace.

His visions indicated Starkad had or at least would come to Ostergotland. Slightly out of the way for Odin's return to Asgard—and he did have pressing business there—but he needed to see to the man. Had he known just how dangerous those vampires were before setting things in motion ... No. The truth was, Odin would still have sent Starkad to retrieve the runeblade, even realizing the danger.

He had no choice. Odin himself could not be in all places at once, nor overcome all foes. He had to use pieces like Starkad if he was to arrange events the way he must in order to win Ragnarok. That weight loomed over Odin's head, ever present, like a dangling sword that followed him no matter which way he turned.

He rode up along the banks of a river until finally coming to an ash tree. Starkad sat beneath it, back pressed up against it, the hood of his cloak up despite the warm weather. Most vampires avoided the sun, but it seemed Starkad felt confident enough in his mortal abilities to care little. Maybe he even welcomed the challenge.

The runeblade lay across Starkad's knees—sheathed—where he ran his fingertips over the hilt. "I thought you would come." The man finally looked up at Odin.

Odin dismounted, hiding his grimace of pain. Starkad knew well enough the true nature of the Aesir and the source of Odin's immortality. Still, it didn't do to show weakness to others—not while appearing as his true self.

"You're really here, in the flesh, aren't you?" Starkad asked. "No dreams, no shadowy, cryptic warnings. No subtle manipulations of my sleeping mind that so oft leave me to believe your schemes are my very own plans. No, you are truly here." Starkad rose, grasping the runeblade's scabbard with one hand. "In the daylight, I cannot hear your heartbeat. But I think you are quite real now."

Odin leaned on his walking stick while Sleipnir wandered off to drink from the river. "I am here, my son."

Starkad snorted. "You are even less a father to me than *he* was."

All Odin could do was shake his head. "Perhaps I deserve your scorn, perhaps not. Either way, I have taken it upon myself to serve as the guardian of all Midgard and all humanity. I rather think that makes me a father to all. Regardless, I did not force you down any of the dark roads you have trod. You may recall I warned you long ago against walking away from the Aesir. Your hubris has guided your every step."

Starkad bared his teeth. In the bright light, his fangs had receded, unnoticeable unless one was looking for them. "You dare speak to me of hubris, old man? Do you know what has happened to me?"

Odin sighed and shook his head once more. He was too weary for this. "I know enough."

"Oh, that I do not doubt. You foresaw all of this, did you not? Perhaps you even planned it from the very beginning. Did you know Hervor would murder my friend? That he would haunt us, destroy us? Did you?"

"Dear Starkad ... you too have the Sight, even if not so strong as mine. Do your instincts predict every outcome with perfect accuracy, years in advance?"

Starkad sneered at him. "I notice you do not answer the question."

Cleverer than he had once been. Time had taught him harsh lessons, it seemed, forced him to grow. Much as it had Odin himself. "You have the only answer I am able to offer you. And you've done well, despite the setbacks you suffered. You helped bring all the runeblades back to the North Realms."

"You used me."

"As you well knew. Your gift had a price."

Now the other man spat at Odin's feet. "I no longer have need of the extra years you've granted me. My death is eternal, as, it seems, is my time upon Midgard."

"Unlikely. Naught lasts forever, as Loki has oft reminded me. Either way, if you wish to be freed from me, just walk away. Only leave the sword."

Starkad chuckled darkly, then slowly slid Mistilteinn from its sheath. A very faint purple light glinted off its runes. "This sword? This blade which can kill even an immortal?" The man pointed the blade at Odin's chest. "Tell me, old man, why should I not kill you for what you have wrought of me? Your hand guided every dark step, every sickening twist of urd that has tormented me until naught remained of the man I was."

Odin took a step back, unable to say with certainty whether Starkad's claims of this runeblade's power held true or not. Each runeblade had its unique, terrible gift. Perhaps any of them might have slain him with enough blows, but Starkad seemed convinced this could do it as though Odin were a mortal man. "The man you were? The man who betrayed his brother?"

"You tricked me!"

"If that were true, you would have struck me down already."

Starkad advanced on him, forcing Odin back until his heels brushed the waters of the river. "I am sore tempted."

Armed with such a blade—if it possessed the power Starkad claimed—the man might just pull it off. Especially considering Odin didn't have Gungnir and was already wounded and exhausted. Still, in daylight, the outcome would've been far from certain. Odin could probably have struck Starkad down and taken the sword.

Neither such a risk nor destroying Starkad actually much served Odin's interest, though. The man had returned the runeblade to the North Realms and was not like to take it far from here. As long as all the runeblades remained in play here, Odin could control them in the end, ensure they wound up where they needed to be come Ragnarok. And indeed, the transformation in Starkad might even serve

Odin's ends. It might have created an even more useful weapon for the final battle.

So Odin held up his hands for peace.

Starkad glared, the debate raging over his face. Then he finally backed away, lowering the runeblade's point into the sand. "Be gone from my sight, Ás. I am no longer your pawn."

Without taking his eyes off Starkad or the fell runeblade, Odin edged along the river to where Sleipnir pranced around. Still watching the vampire, Odin mounted his horse, grunting at the fresh jolt of pain that induced. Then he inclined his hat at Starkad, ever so slightly, turned Sleipnir, and rode out over the river.

Let the man have his momentary victory. After all, Starkad had won it at great price to himself. It had cost him all he had ever loved and even his own life. Odin hardly envied him the pain of it. But then again, Starkad could not imagine the things Odin himself had lost in pursuit of his ends. Such seemed the inevitable price of greatness.

Odin cast a final look back over his shoulder, but Starkad had disappeared off into the trees. He would seek his solitude in the days to come. Some wounds did not heal, of course, but Starkad would no doubt lurk in shadows, hoping for reprieve even as anger and grief festered.

He would, perhaps, think that his transformation might abrogate the curse that had so plagued him.

He would be wrong, of course.

Time would draw him from his solitude and reignite his inevitable wanderlust and need to press human limits. Wars would call him, and Mistilteinn would claim lives again and again.

It all served Odin's aims.

In the meantime, he had a great deal of other pawns that

needed to be guided around the board. The game was far from over.

**The Saga is done for now, but Odin's story continues in**
*The Apples of Idunn*:

https://books2read.com/applesofidunn

SKALDS' TRIBE

Join the Skalds' Tribe and get access to exclusive reader rewards like *The Ragnarok Era Codex*, as well getting free books like *Darkness Forged* and notifications on release dates and sales.

https://www.mattlarkinbooks.com/go-runeblade/

Want maps, character bios, and background information on the Ragnarok Era? Look no further.

# AUTHOR'S RAMBLINGS

Astute readers will note that this book takes place immediately after *The High Seat of Asgard*, with the flashbacks actually occurring during that book. Which is to say, this volume actually brings us up to present in the main *Ragnarok Era* series.

As is my habit, I had this entire series outlined before I even began the first book. As the story developed, in refining the outline and in early drafts, some things changed. Aspects of the tale got expanded, split, or rearranged. One thing that never changed, though, was the ending.

It was inevitable, from the moment Hervor decided to murder Orvar-Oddr, that she would come to a bad end. Her life of violence and murder and amoralism could only end one way. So I knew she would have a terrible fallout with Starkad from the beginning. And naturally, as anyone familiar with the myth knows, she and Höfund would marry and bear a son much more famous than either of them.

So yes, this is the end of the series, at least in its present arc. If time allows and the demand is there, I could continue it later in the timeline. Hervor's son Heidrik has his own share of dark adventures that I would very much enjoy retelling some day.

Also worth noting is that in Starkad's original myth, he gets his jaw cut off by a different shieldmaiden in a different battle (Vebiorg, in fact). However, the story demanded it unequivocally be Hervor. How could it be anyone else?

Special thanks to my wife, to my cover designer, to my editor, to Lisa, and to everyone in the Skalds' Tribe for supporting me in this project.

Thank you for reading,
Matt

P.S. Reviews are super important, especially to small presses like mine. Without reviews, small presses cannot get ads. It takes only a single line or two to make that difference. So if you liked this, please leave a review where you bought it!

Want to talk about the book? I'd love to hear from you. You can reach me at: matt@mattlarkinbooks.com

# BOOKS BY MATT LARKIN

### Gods of the Ragnarok Era

The Ragnarok Era is a dark fantasy retelling of Norse mythology, chronicling Odin's rise to godhood. If you love old legends, tragic mythology, and action-packed reads, check out The Ragnarok Era now!

https://www.mattlarkinbooks.com/series/ragnarok/

### Legends of the Ragnarok Era

Legends of the Ragnarok Era expands on the world developed in The Ragnarok Era series by delivering dark tales outside the main series narrative. Fans of mythology should not miss this epic series.

https://www.mattlarkinbooks.com/series/ragnaroklegend/

### Runeblade Saga

The Runeblade Saga is a series of dark fantasy sword and sorcery adventures set in the world of The Ragnarok Era. Filled with plenty of grim action, tragic heroes, and more than a bit of horror, these books are for fans of mythology and sword & sorcery alike.

https://www.mattlarkinbooks.com/series/runeblade/

*For Juhi. Thank you.*

Made in the USA
Columbia, SC
21 April 2020